Citrus

of Oz

Lizy J Campbell

Dedicated to everyone and anyone who
needs a little escape from reality

"Is this a trial of thoughts, or of kit-
tens?" demanded the Woggle-Bug.
'It's a trial of one kitten,' replied the
Scarecrow; 'but your manner is a trial to us
all."
— L. Frank Baum, Ozma of Oz

Disclaimer: There are some intense sex scenes and discussions about a miscarriage within. This is an adult fantasy fiction, sci-fi story. It's just a bit of fun fantasy for those who love to bend reality. I will not apologize for my creative freedom. I hope you enjoy the story arc and characters. Think Bridgerton romance meets outer space. This is my very first romance book that I have written. Enjoy!

Chapters

Prologue

The control panel lit up in a blur of red, yellow, and orange. The size of the planet became increasingly closer to impact. My hands flew over the switches and dials. My breath is shallow and in short bursts as my panic rises.

Outside the reinforced window of my small spacecraft, the black void of space illuminated by a chaotic storm of solar flares, a brilliant white light twisted and writhed, making the interior of my ship glow.

"This wasn't supposed to happen," I mutter frantically, scanning the panels of my console. "This planet isn't even on the systems maps!"

A golden yellow-hued planet in the distance appears almost serene, in contrast to the raging storm of hot flames that now threatens to tear my ship apart as it shakes. I had been en route to a refueling station when a massive solar storm erupted out of nowhere, something I'd never encountered quite like it this

The ship jolts violently, throwing me against the straps of my harness. It's sending pain signals to my brain. A sudden, loud crack echoes through the cabin as a panel splits open, spraying sparks like a fountain of streaking stars on the interior wall. My heart pounds in my chest as I fight to regain control, thankful that I decided to put on my helmet just moments before the storm began.

"Mayday! Mayday! This is Lieutenant Dotty Gates of the U.S.S. Kansas, requesting immediate assistance. There's significant ship damage, and I am running out of oxygen!" I shout into the comms, but only static answers my call. The storm has now severed the link to my home base and this ship. I realize now that no one can hear me respond.

The navigational systems are flickering and nonresponsive, and manual control is impossible with the turbulence rocking the vessel. I have to land this metal ball of fire or crash it into this planet before the ship disintegrates.

I grit my teeth and yank as hard as I can on the manual controls, steering the ship toward a green area that seems soft enough for a crash landing. The ship's descent quickens, and the planet's atmosphere turns the air outside the window into a blazing inferno, starting to melt the metal exterior. My watering eyes dart to the altimeter as it spins in a blur of numbers: 10,000 feet, 8,000 feet, 6,000 feet.

I brace myself just before the ship slams fast into the ground with a deafening roar. The impact throws me forward, snapping the harness tight across my chest. For a moment, everything is chaos, metal screeching, glass shattering, and my world goes black

Hours later, I wake up groggy, sweaty, and disoriented. The ship is upside down, its nose buried in the planet's soft ground. I unlatch the harness and fall to the ceiling, now the floor. Pain shoots through my shoulders from the impact. After checking myself, I find no fatal injuries, but I have many cuts, bruises, and scrapes. My helmet is cracked, and my uniform is torn with blackened smoke stains.

The ship is a wreck, twisted and mangled beyond recognition. Smoke fills the cabin, and the scent of burning electronics stings my nose. I cough and gag, struggling to breathe. I grab my emergency pack and stumble toward the gaping hole in the hatch where it used to be. It takes all my strength to walk there; the metal groans in protest as I step carefully to avoid a weak spot in the ship that could cause me to fall through.

I step outside, my boots sinking into the soft, fragrant ground. The helmet I'm wearing isn't protecting me from the air now. I slip it off and breathe in deeply. If I am going to die, I'd rather it be quick.

The air is thick and sweet. It's filled with the scent of citrus. The sky above is an electric yellow, tinged with green clouds. Massive, fruit-like trees surround me, their leaves shimmering with an iridescent light. The fruit here seems to glow slightly. I wait for my breathing to labor, to pass out until my death, but I don't.

I take in my surroundings, and the silence is unnerving. It's broken only by the distant hum of an unseen energy.

I am alive, but I am stranded.

In the distance, there is a faint light flickering among the trees. A beacon? A settlement? Hope stirs in me. I grab the pack that I thankfully found amongst the ship's rubble. I hold onto it tightly; it's the only thing left connecting me to home.

Chapter 1

Rusty joy

I push through the dense underbrush, each step filling my boots with the strange, soft earth of the planet, which feels spongy beneath me. The sweet citrus scent hangs heavy in the air, mingling with the faint smell of burning wires on my flight suit. The light in the distance pulses rhythmically, like a heartbeat, guiding me deeper into the alien landscape.

I am unsure how long I have been walking; time feels distorted on this planet, the sky shifting between hues of yellow and green without warning. I push my dark charcoal black hair away and out of my bright blue eyes, my bangs cling to the sweat on my forehead from the heavy moisture in the atmosphere. My mind races with questions, and I wonder if anyone will come looking for me here. But how could they? I didn't even know this place existed until now. I don't want to think about my anxiety rising and making me dizzy. I push it out of my mind.

I push through a cluster of tall, glowing ferns and hear a faint, metallic clanking off in the distance. I freeze, my hand instinctively reaching for the laser cutter I took out of my pack and have clipped onto my belt. The sound of clanking grows louder, accompanied by a whirring noise, like gears turning in need of oil.

Carefully, I step forward, parting the ferns to reveal a small clearing. In the center stands a peculiar figure, a rusted, robotic dog. The dog's metal body is scratched and dented; patches of its once-shiny surface are dulled by years of exposure to the elements. One of its ears is missing, it looks like it was patched up at some point, as there are different colored pieces of metal. It's funny looking tail twitches sporadically, emitting a faint spark every time it moves closer to me.

The dog notices me. It tilts its head. The whirring sound paused as if it were assessing me. I hold my breath, unsure if the robot is friendly or hostile.

The dog lets out a soft, tin bark and trots over to me, its movements jerky but full of eagerness. It circles my legs, wagging its tail erratically before sitting down and looking at me inquisitively with its head tilted.

"Hey there," I kneeled to get a closer look. The dog's stance brightens, and it lets out another mechanical bark.

I reach out to touch it, and the dog leans into my hand, its metal surface warm from the sunlight filtering through the trees. I notice a small panel on its side with faded lettering that reads: *Model: T.O.T.O. - Tactical Operations Terrain Observer.*

My immediate thoughts and impression are that this creature is both out of place and perfectly at home in the alien wilderness of Citria. The robotic dog stood sturdy. A compact build, his exterior a polished composite that gleamed slightly under Citria's four suns. His design was sleek, hinting at advanced technology with every contour and joint engineered for agility and durability.

My initial surprise quickly morphed into fascination as I observed the mechanical canine. *There was an instant charm about T.O.T.O., his movements fluid and precise, exuding a sense of purpose and intelligence. Despite his mechanical nature, there is something undeniably lifelike and endearing about him. I feel relief and excitement. A companion in this vast, unfamiliar world could make all the difference. His presence promised not just company, but a layer of security in the unpredictable wilderness of Citria.*

"T.O.T.O, huh? Well, aren't you just a cute little guy?" I say with a smile. "What are you doing out here all alone?"

The dog responds with beeps and whirs, as if trying to communicate with me. It then turns and looks toward the distant light I have been following; its metal tail keeps wagging.

"You want to go there too?" I ask myself more than for the dog. T.O.T.O. barks in response, its tail wagging faster.

"All right, T.O.T.O.," standing up. "Lead the way, let's see what's waiting for us."

T.O.T.O barks excitedly and bounds ahead, leading through some thick foliage.

***

Dotty follows, the two of them moving together, their odd partnership already forming a bond.

Dotty notices that T.O.T.O. is more than just an outdated model; he has a personality, a spark of curiosity and determination that reminds her of her old copilot, a real dog she had lost long ago. The robot dog stops frequently to inspect the strange flora, sniffing at the glowing fruits hanging from the trees, and sometimes nudging her to look at it, but only if it finds something interesting.

The light in the distance grows brighter as they near, its pulsing rhythm quickening. Dotty takes a deep breath. She loves the smell of the lemons; it reminds her so much of home and her aunts' garden.

Chapter 2

The graveyard

We venture deeper into the strange wilderness, following the pulse of the distant light. The landscape gradually shifts, the lush greenery giving way to a barren, cracked earth.

The sweet citrus scent in the air fades, replaced by a metallic tang that clings to the back of my throat and makes me want to gag as the smell is dense. The once vibrant sky has dulled to a sickly, rotten orange, casting long shadows that flicker with an eerie, unnatural glow.

My unease grows with every step, and T.O.T.O.'s whirs and clicks take on a wary edge as they move through this increasingly desolate terrain. Once full of glowing yellow and green fruit trees, they now stand twisted and barren, their branches reaching toward the sky like skeletal fingers trying to escape the carnage. The ground is littered with debris. There are fragments of metal, shards of glass, and something else that makes my stomach turn: pieces of broken, decaying life forms, I know not of what they are.

I slow my pace, scanning the area. The sentient beings lay scattered across the landscape in varying states of destruction. Some are merely hollow shells, their vibrant orange flesh withered and shrunken. Others are torn apart, their insides spilled across the ground in a mess of seeds and strange, pulpy material that glistens under the waning light.

It is as if I have stumbled upon a battlefield grave, the remnants of a terrible conflict that has long since ended. But the air is thick with a sense of foreboding, as if the battle's echoes still linger, waiting to ensnare the unwary.

"What happened here?" I whisper to myself. The robotic dog stays close to my side, tail lowered as it scans the area with bright blue eyes.

As we walk, I notice something odd about the bodies and how they are scattered. They aren't haphazardly strewn about; rather, they are arranged in deliberate patterns, as if someone, or something, placed them there. The bodies form strange symbols, concentric circles, and spirals that spiral outward across the cracked earth. Each symbol pulses with a faint, sickly light, as if still clinging to the last vestiges of life.

T.O.T.O whines softly, drawing my attention to a particularly large cluster of broken the dead near the edge of the clearing. I approached cautiously, my hand resting on the hilt of the laser cutter now strapped to my belt. I can see that these aliens are different from the others. Their rinds are a darker, almost blood-red hue, and their faces, once full of malevolent energy, are frozen in expressions of terror and anguish.

The sight sends a shiver down my spine. These species haven't just died; they have been destroyed; their very essence ripped apart. But for what? Or by whom?

A sudden, raspy breath breaks the silence, causing me to whip around. My heart pounds as I search for the source of the sound. I look and land on a lone figure slumped against a nearby boulder. Unlike the others, this one is still alive, barely. The body is mangled, its rind torn and leaking thick, dark juice that pools around it like blood. The body is dim, flickering as I approach.

"T.O.T.O, stay close," I say quietly, my voice tight with caution. The robotic dog moves to my side; its sensors trained on the dying creature.

I crouch down beside it, my gaze locking with it. The creature's breath rattles in its chest, each exhaling a painful wheeze. It tries to speak, but only a garbled sound comes out, more of a croak than a voice.

"What happened here?" leaning closer. "Who did this to you?"

The being struggles to lift its head, its mouth twisting into a grotesque grin. "You… shouldn't… be here…" it rasps, each word a struggle.

My heart hammers in my chest as the warning slices through the eerie stillness of the graveyard-like clearing. With each painful, gasping word, its twisted form fires warning signs. Everything in me wants to run away from here.

"You shouldn't be here..." The words hang heavily in the air, laden with an ominous weight that tightens around my heart like a vice.

My instincts are screaming as I lean in. Yet I am driven by this insatiable need for answers.

"What do you mean?" I press the creature further, trying to make sense of the message.

The alien's body shudders. "The light, the Zest… you follow…" It coughs, a wet, choking sound, as more dark black juice dribbles from its mouth. "It is not what it seems…"

I feel the tiny hairs on the back of my neck rise. "What do you mean? What's the Zest?"

Its eyes glaze over, its body going limp. I think it has died, but then it speaks one last time, its voice barely a whisper.

"The Zest… is a lie… Beware… the light…"

With that, the body dims completely. Its body collapsing into a heap. The strange, dark juice seeps into the cracked earth, leaving nothing but shriveled husk behind.

I stare at the lifeless remains, my mind racing. What had it meant? The Zest was a lie? And the light, the beacon I had been following, was something to beware of? The words echo in my mind, filling me with a growing dread.

T.O.T.O lets out a low whine, nudging my leg with his nose. I reach down and pat the dog's metal head, trying to calm myself and it.

"We need to keep moving," I say, my voice sounding uncertain. "Whatever's out there, it's not friendly, I suspect, and we must not be found by whatever it is."

But as I stand and gaze toward the distant light, now tinged with an ominous red glow, I can't shake the feeling that the dying are a warning that was more than just the ramblings of a creature on the brink of death.

***

The field of the fallen bodies felt like a graveyard, haunted by the echoes of a forgotten war. T.O.T.O. and I moved through it, the strange symbols glowing faintly under their feet. Every step felt heavier than the last, as if the ground itself was pulling them down, urging them to join the ranks of the dead.

As we walk, my thoughts churn. What was this "Zest" it had mentioned? A power source? A weapon? And why did it involve the light I had been so determined to reach? I wasn't sure what lay ahead, but one thing was certain: the path forward was far more dangerous than she had imagined.

The planet of Citria was full of secrets, and the deeper she ventured, the darker they became. T.O.T.O's sensors suddenly flared, a series of urgent beeps breaking the silence.

I looked down to see the dog focused on something in the distance, a glimmer of movement among the debris. I tense, ready to draw my laser cutter, but then I see a faint, wavering figure moving toward them. At first, I thought it was another alien, but as the figure drew closer, I realized it was different. It was taller, more humanoid, its body clad in tattered robes that fluttered in the breeze. Face obscured by a hood, but from beneath the shadows, a pair of glowing yellow dots for eyes peered into her soul.

I took a step back, my hand tightening around my weapon. "Who are you?" I demand, trying to keep my voice steady. The figure stops, standing still among the wreckage.

For a moment, it said nothing, observing me. Then, in a voice that seemed to echo from the very air. It spoke.

"I am the Guardian of the Fallen," it said, its tone calm yet laced with sorrow. "I watch over those who have perished in the name of the Zest."

I swallowed hard.

The Guardian stands solemnly before me; his presence is almost ethereal amidst the vibrant foliage of the alien landscape. His skin, the rich yellow of a ripe lemon, seemed to radiate a soft glow, casting a warm, inviting light in the cooler shades of the forest. This luminous hue was not just striking but seemed an integral part of his be-ing, as if his very essence was intertwined with the citrus heart of the planet itself. The creature's eyes were deep and wise, held millennia of knowledge, shimmering like twin stars caught within his lemon-yellow stature. Tall and imposing yet exuding a gentle calm.

"What happened here? Why are all these beings… dead?"

The Guardian's mouth twitches with mischief. "They were trying to destroy us," he says. "They were led to their doom by the one they trusted most."

My heart pounded in my chest. "But what is the Zest? The alien said it was a lie."

The Guardian's mood changes. "The Zest is not a tangible thing to achieve. It is a legend woven by those who crave power. It is said to grant untold strength, to bring life to the barren, and heal the wounded. But it is a curse, a deception that leads only to destruction."

I suddenly feel cold. "And the light, the beacon I've been following?"

The Guardian's gaze turns toward the distant glow, now throbbing with a dark, foreboding energy. "The light, which is the orb, is the main hold in which we are protected from the Tangarmarine army," he says, voice heavy with the weight of ancient knowledge. "It is our last defense against their relentless assault."

My mind races as I try to process the Guardian's words.

The Guardian nods to the orb. "The Tangarmarines were once our kin. Born from the same soil, they were twisted and blinded by a

Sorceress. She corrupted them with her lies and promises of power. They turned against us, seeking to consume all that we hold dear. The light in the distance is our sanctuary, the last bastion of hope for the Citrusians."

I feel my spine stiffen. The dying Tangarmarine's warning now takes on a new, terrifying significance.

If the light was the only thing protecting the Citrusians from the Tangarmarines, it wasn't just a beacon. It was a fortress, a shield against a malevolent force I had barely begun to understand.

"But if the light is a hold, why did that Tangarmarine say the Zest is a lie?" I ask, my voice trembling with confusion. "What is this Zest it mentioned?"

The Guardian's expression grew somber, its glowing eyes dim with sorrow. "The Zest is fictitious. It is not what the Tangamarines believe it to be. The Orb is the essence of our world and the life force that sustains all living things in Citria. We have yet to discover its full power. The Citrusians guard it and protect it. The mayor foretold in ancient scrolls that the Orb was the key to our survival. The Tangamarrines, driven mad by the Sorceress's magic and manipulation, seek to take it for themselves, believing it will grant them unimaginable power."

My pulse quickened. "So, the Tangarmarines are trying to steal the Zest, or sorry, the Orb? To take it for themselves to rule this planet?"

"Yes," the Guardian replied, its voice tinged with regret. "They believe the Zest, as they call it, will give them dominion over all of Citria. Making them invincible. But they do not understand its true nature. The orb is a delicate balance, a harmony that sustains all life on this planet. To tamper with it, to take it by force, would be to destroy everything."

My mind is spinning as I consider the implications. The light I had been following was not just a beacon of hope, a line of defense, a last stand against a relentless enemy. And the orb is the very essence of life on this planet.

"I just want to go home, is that possible?" I ask, my voice barely above a whisper. "Can anyone help me get off this planet?"

The Guardian's gaze softens, but the tone remains resolute. "I understand your longing to return home, Dotty. But the path to your world lies through the light. If you wish to leave this planet, you must help the Citrusians protect the orb and stop the Tangamarines from unleashing chaos upon Citria. Only then can the way be opened."

My heart sank. I had hoped for an easier answer, a simple solution that would whisk me back to the safety of my home. But the Guardian's words made it clear that my fate is now entwined with that of this alien world

"If I do this… if I help … will I be able to go home?"

The Guardian's glowing eyes held mine with an intensity that made my breath catch. "The light holds many secrets, and the Zest possesses great power. If you succeed, the Citrusians will do everything to help you return home."

I nod, though fear is gnawing at me inside. I hadn't signed up for this fight, but there was no other choice. My only hope of returning home is to press forward, to reach the light and face whatever awaits me there.

"All right," my voice steadier now. "I'll do whatever it takes."

The Guardian's expression was unreadable. There was a sense of approval, its light flared briefly before dimming. "Then go, Dotty. Follow the light, and may you find the strength to fulfill your destiny."

The Guardian began glowing brighter. "The path ahead is fraught with danger. The light will guide you, and the Citrusians will welcome you as an ally once you reach it. But beware, there is a Sorceress and her Tangarmarine army, they will stop at nothing to claim the Zest. I do hope that you can save us all."

With those words, the Guardian's form shimmered and faded into the air, leaving me alone with T.O.T.O. in the silent field of the fallen.

***

The path ahead was fraught with danger, but I knew what I had to do. I felt a surge of determination, but also a growing gnawing sense of fear. I was just a pilot, after all, stranded on a strange planet I barely understood.

T.O.T.O, sensing my concern, let out a low bark, his tail wagging in encouragement.

I smile faintly, grateful for his companionship. "I'll do it, what other choice do I have." Squaring my shoulders. I take a deep breath and start forward, T.O.T.O by my side.

The path ahead was uncertain, but I knew I couldn't turn back now. The fate of Citria, and even my own, depended on what lay at the end of this journey. As we moved toward the light, the ground beneath their feet crackled with energy, the symbols etched into the earth glowing faintly in response to their presence.

***

The closer they got to the light, the more Dotty could feel a strange warmth, a sense of power thrumming in the air. It was as if the orb was alive, aware of their approach.

But with that warmth came a growing sense of dread, a dark cloud that seemed to hang over the landscape. The Tangarmarine was an army out there, lurking in the shadows, waiting for the right moment to strike.

And the Sorceress, Dotty, could almost feel a presence of a cold, malevolent force that sent shivers down her spine. The battlefield for Citria was far from being over.

Chapter 3

The code please

The landscape beyond the old battlefield of Citria unfolds like a vibrant woven tapestry.

The terrain is a complex amalgamation of crystalline plains, glowing fruit, and lush valleys and forests.

Towering mountains with jagged, iridescent peaks dominate the horizon, their bases shrouded in a mist that glows faintly under its four suns. These mountains function as natural fortresses, harboring secrets from the planet. Between these giants lie expansive forests, where the soil sparkles with a slight luminescence. This glow intensifies in the twilight hours, creating pathways of light that guide the nocturnal creatures.

From the sky, graceful beings resembling giant bioluminescent butterflies soar, their wings casting colorful light. They cast glowing shadows on the ground below, much like fireflies, but much bigger.

On the ground, sentient flora coexist with ambulatory species, some of whom have developed symbiotic relationships, critical for survival.

One such example is the glimmering Tendrilaxadia. A plant-animal hybrid, harmless with a tiny array of colored spots, orange to deep pinks and greens, depending on the location on the planet. The species itself is so small that it is often unseen by travelers.

The foliage on Citria defies the conventions of earthly plants. Here, the flora pulsates with life, exhibiting slow, rhythmic movements that suggest a kind of primitive sentience.

The striking features are the yellow star leaflet clusters and hanging and glowing lemon-looking fruit. Some cousin plants grow along the streams and water bodies. Often, bare no fruit. Their leaves are broad and shimmering with a spectrum of colors, photosynthesize light from Citria's weak suns with incredible efficiency.

During the day, these leaves fold inward, capturing and storing energy, only to unfurl at night in a spectacular display of light and color, illuminating the landscape in a dance of hues that mirrors the starlit sky above.

The soil is rich with bioluminescent fungi and other microorganisms, which form a network of glowing patterns, often seen tracing the roots of trees and creating a natural guide through the darker recesses of the forests.

Despite the beautiful landscape toward the light, it feels more treacherous as Dotty and T.O.T.O press on.

T.O.T.O trots ahead, his sensors alert as he scouts the way forward. The robotic dog's presence is a comfort, a reminder that she wasn't entirely alone. The light they follow flickers in the distance, like a far-off star beckoning them closer.

The air crackles with static, and the occasional gust of wind carries the faint scent of citrus, mingled with something more metallic, like the sharp tang of soldered wires.

Dotty's thoughts are still tangled with the cryptic words of the Guardian.

She had agreed to help the Citrusians protect the orbs, to reach the light, and join them in their final stand against the Tangarmarines. But as much as she tries to focus on the task, the longing to return home gnaws at her.

As they rounded a bend in the path, Dotty's attention was drawn to a peculiar sight: a tall figure standing motionless in the middle of a field.

The figure imposing is seven feet tall, with a slender yet sturdy frame composed of weathered wood intertwined with rusty metal. The structure of its body, a marvel of design, mimics human anatomy but is mechanical. Intricate gears and pistons were partially exposed beneath the patchwork of his outer layers, giving him a skeletal yet robust form.

His head is particularly striking. It is crafted from an old, sack-like material stretched taut over a rigid frame to create a face shape. Deep-set eyes, glowing with a soft, yellow light, sit beneath what might have been a brow if he were human.

These eyes give him a watchful, eerie gaze that seems to pierce through the shadows of the forest, where a mouth would be, instead, interlocking metal plates shifting and moving as he simulates speech, enhancing his otherworldly demeanor.

Its attire adds to his charm, yet it remains futuristic in appearance. He wears a long, flowing coat made entirely from a patchwork of old, tattered fabrics. The colors are faded, blended of dark yellow and grey with the occasional shimmer of metal and circuitry that catches the light, depending on the angle. Around his neck, twisted cords and wires are fashioned into a makeshift scarf, dangling loosely and swaying with his movements.

A belt around his waist, which looked to house various tools and devices, a small energy scanner, and a multi-tool with numerous fold-out mechanisms. It had a compact data pad illuminated with complex glyphs on its chest.

Dotty approaches cautiously, her hand resting on the hilt of her laser cutter. T.O.T.O's sensors hummed as he scanned the figure, his tail wagging slightly as he determined it posed no immediate threat.

The figure remains still as Dotty and T.O.T.O draw nearer.

***

"Hello?" I call out, my voice echoing in the still air. "Can you hear me?"

The figure's eyes flickered to life, glowing a dull yellow as it turned its head toward me. It was staring, as if trying to process her presence. Then, with a creak of rusty joints, it spoke.

"Greetings, traveler," the figure said in a voice that buzzed and crackled like a faulty speaker from an old FM radio. "I am the Scarecrow, a sentinel of the fields that protect their crops. But my purpose… my programming… it is incomplete."

I blink in surprise. "Incomplete? What do you mean?"

The Scarecrow thought briefly, as if contemplating its response. "I was created to protect the fields from intruders," it explained, its voice a mixture of confusion and frustration. "But my creators... they abandoned me before they could complete my programming. I lack... intelligence. The knowledge to understand, I think, is for myself. I have spent countless cycles standing here, waiting. Hoping for someone to upgrade my programming."

I feel sorry for the Scarecrow. I know all too well what it feels like to be stranded.

"What kind of upgrade are you looking for?" I ask out of curiosity.

The Scarecrow's eyes brightened. "I require an upgrade to my cognitive processors," it says. "An infusion of intelligence, a way to expand my programming so that I may understand more than simple commands. I wish to think, to learn, to be... intelligent."

I glance at T.O.T.O., who was watching the Scarecrow. "And what happens if you get this upgrade? What will you do then?"

The Scarecrow hesitated, its gaze shifting to the distant light on the horizon. "I do not know," it admitted. "But I hope… that I will find purpose. I will no longer be a sentinel standing idle, but something greater."

I consider the Scarecrow's words.

"Well," I said, "I'm heading toward that light in the distance. I don't know if I can help you with an upgrade, but perhaps we can find someone there who can."

The Scarecrow smiles a flicker of hope. "The light… it is a beacon, yes? A source of knowledge?"

I nod in agreement. "I think so. At least, that's what I've been told. It's where the Citrusians are making their stand against the Tangarmarines. If there's anywhere you might find what you're looking for, it's there."

The Scarecrow considered this, its head tilting slightly as if weighing the possibilities. Then, with a creak of metal and a hiss of steam, it took a step forward. "If permitted, I will accompany you, traveler," it says.

I smile. "Glad to have you with us. My name's Dotty, and this is T.O.T.O."

The Scarecrow nodded stiffly. "Logic is my compass, curiosity my fuel, and every mystery is a map to discover. Dotty and T.O.T.O., let us proceed toward the light, but I am afraid I have gotten rusty, so it will take some time to loosen my joints."

"Fair enough, Scarecrow, we can go at your pace until you feel better."

Scarecrow's clanking footsteps echo alongside my quieter steps and T.O.T.O's soft whir as we follow the glowing light beyond. "I am not sure we will be quiet enough to sneak up on anyone, should we need to." I laugh.

Scarecrow looks at me and chuckles, "Indeed, Dotty."

The orbs' glow casts a long, eerie shadow across the landscape. The air buzzes with a low hum, like the sound of distant machinery or faint crackling of energy.

I notice the Scarecrow occasionally tilting its head as if listening to something only it could hear. It would pause momentarily before continuing.

"So, Scarecrow," I say, "what do you remember about your creators? Who built you?"

The Scarecrow processes the question. "I believe my creators were engineers of the Citrusians," its voice softer now, almost nostalgic.

"As time passed, I wondered if I could complete myself. If I could somehow find the upgrade, I need to think for myself, to become… more than just a sentinel."

"I think you're already more than just a sentinel," giving a reassuring smile. "You've been searching for a way to improve yourself, to find your purpose. Some struggle within my world, even those with all the intelligence."

The Scarecrow looked up, "Your words… resonate with me. With your help, I can finally achieve what I seek."

The twisted remnants of machinery and the occasional sparking wire hint at a once-thriving world now caught in the grip of decay all around them. But as we walk, I begin to notice something strange. The light ahead was changing, growing more intensely and more erratically. The steady pulse that had guided them was now a rapid flicker, as if the light was struggling to stay alive.

"Something's wrong," I murmur, my eyes narrowing as I study the glow. "It's like the light is… faltering."

The Scarecrow turned its gaze toward the light, its sensors whirring as it analyzed the situation. "The energy output is fluctuating," it observed. "There may be a disruption at the source. We should proceed with caution."

I nodded, "Agreed. We don't know what we're walking into."

As they approached the light, the air grew thick with tension. The ground beneath their feet began trembling, and the once-quiet hum of machinery escalated into a discordant cacophony. I could feel the energy all around us, a powerful force pulsing through the air we breathe. But it was unstable, volatile, like a storm waiting to break.

Finally, we crest a rise, and the source of the light comes into view. My breath catches in my throat.

In the center of a vast, crater-like clearing stood a massive, glowing orb suspended in mid-air by a network of cables and machinery. The orb radiating a blinding yellow and green light, its surface crackling with arcs.

I look down and see a massive, vast, and dense forest with a yellow-dusted sand pathway that is cut right down the middle of it. I feel a pang of sadness. It's the lonely part of me, now deeply rooted in my longing for home. I ache with every step.

"That looks like where we need to go, let's follow that yellow sand road." My voice broke as I held back the tears, not wanting the others to see, turning my back on them and beginning to walk out front.   follows behind, and T.O.T.O sniffs things off in the bushes.

I take a deep breath, "Come on, T.O.T.O., and Scarecrow, it's time to embrace the unknown. One step, one breath, and one brave leap into this wonderous place in time."

Chapter 4

Home is where the heart is

Growing up under the care of my Aunt and Uncle, I always felt a bit like a wildflower. I was planted by chance, thriving on the unexpected. My mom died giving birth to me, so they took me in. I never knew about my dad either, nobody ever talked about him. I guess that's for another story and another lifetime.

My caregivers weren't the conventional type, seasoned engineers. Their lives were a tapestry of interstellar assignments and cosmic adventure, which meant my childhood was anything but ordinary.

Our home was either at a space station or a spaceship when duty called. That lifestyle taught me to adapt, to find home wherever we were, planting gardens of memories all the time. Despite their demanding careers, they always carved out time for me, their schedules meticulously organized around my school modules and, later, my budding interests in mechanics and astrophysics.

They weren't just my guardians. They were my first teachers who stoked the fires of curiosity in my mind. I was their little assistant, and right from the start, as soon as I was old enough, I handed them tools as they worked on various engineering projects. These moments, filled with the scent of ionized metal and the sound of their harmonious banter over circuit diagrams, became my playground of happiness.

Their love was practical. It was profoundly expressed through lessons on gravity fields rather than bedtime stories. They taught me resilience in the face of cosmic storms and the importance of precise calculations, both in engineering and in life decisions. Every lesson was an adventure, and every challenge was a puzzle solved together.

But it wasn't all equations and experiments. Some evenings were our time for softer moments. We'd gather on the viewing deck, watching stars and telling each other make-believe stories about the constellations.

My uncle would point out the technicalities of space travel, while my aunt would spin silly tales of mythical creatures believed to roam the less explored planets. These stories, rich with adventure and wonder, filled my dreams and ambitions with an eager longing for exploration.

When I built my first drone, they celebrated its successful launch as if it were my rite of passage. And even when it crashed, they were there with smiles and soldering irons, ready to help me put it back together.

Theirs was a world where science was the language of love, and innovation the currency of care. I thrived on it.

I was born and raised off and on board the U.S.S. Kansas, a mid-sized but well-equipped starship that served as a hub for refueling and repairs for various spacecraft navigating the busy trade routes near the outer colonies.

Kansas was more than just a technical outpost; it was a vibrant community in orbit, home to families and individuals from various corners of the galaxy, providing a melting pot of cultures and ideas that shaped my upbringing.

I've just turned 20, and my body is in good physical condition. My athletic build comes from all the training in zero-gravity environments, or good genetics. My hair is a vivid shade of auburn, typically pulled back into a tight ponytail that suits the practical necessities of space travel.

My decision to undertake the routine refueling mission was driven by my desire to prove to myself that I was capable of managing tasks typically reserved for more experienced crew members.

The mission was supposed to be straightforward: travel to a nearby depot, collect the fuel, and return. It was a chance to demonstrate my skills and assert my independence, highlighting my readiness for more significant responsibilities. I wanted to prove to my aunt and uncle how capable I was. But now that I am stuck on this planet, I don't feel like proving much of anything. I just wanted to see their faces again, to be home in the warmth of their presence.

Chapter 5

Half man, Half robot

The air was thick with the scent of ozone and decaying foliage, and the trees towered above like silent sentinels, their leaves a deep shade of emerald that shimmered in the faint light. The forest floor was littered with fallen branches and strange, twisted roots that seemed to pulse with a faint yellowish glow, like veins carrying life-blood through the alien earth.

T.O.T.O., the Scarecrow, and I walk cautiously along the winding trail, the dense canopy above casting long shadows that danced and shifted with every step. Following the light, it was now obscured by the thick foliage. But I could still feel its presence. The air was cooler here, almost refreshing compared to the oppressive heat of the open plains, but an undercurrent of unease that was keeping me on edge.

The Scarecrow moves with surprising agility for something so tall and gangly, its metal joints creaking softly with every step. I could see the wear and tear on its body more clearly now—rust eating away at its joints, wires exposed and frayed, and patches of metal that looked like they had been hastily repaired. It was a wonder the Scarecrow was still functioning at all.

T.O.T.O's sensors flick and hum as he scans the surroundings, his tail wagging in a steady rhythm as he moves ahead of me. Suddenly, he stops, his ears perking up as he catches an unfamiliar low, metallic groan, followed by the clanking of heavy footsteps. I freeze; my heart is racing as I strain to listen.

"Did you hear that?" I whisper, glancing at the Scarecrow.

The Scarecrow nods, its glowing eyes narrowing as it scans the area. "Yes. It sounds like… another machine. But different. Heavier."

The noise grows louder, and I can make out the unmistakable sound of metal grinding against metal, accompanied by labored breathing, if it could be called that. The sound was coming from deep within the forest, off the main path. Curiosity mingled with caution as I gestured for T.O.T.O to stay close. I turn toward the source, moving carefully through the underbrush, the shaking Scarecrow following close behind.

As we push through a thicket of thorny vines, I finally catch sight of the source of the noise. In a small clearing, surrounded by towering trees, there is a figure unlike anything I have ever seen. It is a Cyborg, a fusion of a younger man and machine, but time had not been kind to it. Its metal parts were corroded, patches of rust spreading like a disease across its body. The organic parts were no better. Its skin looked bruised and dirty, and one human and one metal eye flickered weakly in its socket, its glow dim and fading.

The Cyborg was hunched over, struggling to move, every step a painful effort. His joints creak with each movement. The sound of labored breathing came from a mechanical chest cavity that wheezed with every intake of air, as if the Cyborg's existence was an ongoing battle against inevitable decay.

The Cyborg looks like it is struggling, and there is something in its eye, something desperate or a flicker of determination.

The Cyborg, with its blend of male human features and advanced robotics, is unlike anything on the U.S.S. Kansas. Something about him seems to represent the pinnacle of engineering fusion of technology and humanity that resonated deeply with me.

"Hello?" I call out softly, taking a cautious step forward. "Are you okay?"

The Cyborg's head jerks up at the sound of my voice, its one eye locking onto me. It stares momentarily, as if trying to determine whether I was real or just another figment of its deteriorating sensors. Then, it speaks.

"Who… who are you?" the Cyborg rasps, its voice a harsh, metallic whisper. "What… what do you want?"

"My name is Dotty," I reply, keeping my voice calm and steady. "I'm just passing through. I saw you and thought you might need help."

The Cyborg's eye flickers again, letting out a sound that might have been a laugh if it weren't so painful. "Help?… there's no helping me. Not unless you can… give me a new energy core."

My eyebrows furrow. "An energy core?"

The Cyborg nods in agreement, its head moving stiffly. "My core… It's failing, worn out. I've been searching… searching for a replacement, but… no luck. I'm running on fumes. It won't be long before… I shut down for good."

I feel sympathy for this creature as I did for T.O.T.O. The Cyborg needed assistance.

"I'm sorry," I say, my voice tinged with re-gret. "I don't have an energy core to give you. But maybe if we reach the light, we can find something there. It's where I'm headed, and it might have what you need."

The Cyborg's eye narrows as it takes in those words carefully. "The light... the beacon? You're... you're going there?"

I nod. "Yes. I'm trying to reach it. I am confident it should have the resources to help you."

The Cyborg let out another wheezing breath, its shoulders slumping as if the weight of its situation was finally sinking in. "I've been... wandering for so long. So long, trying to... hold on, lost. But... if you're going to the light, maybe... I can make it there too. Maybe... it'll have a core for me."

"Come with us," My voice firm. "We'll help you get to the light. We'll find you that core."

The Cyborg's eye flickers slowly. "Thank you... Dotty. I'll... I'll try to keep up. But... I'm not as fast as I used to be."

The Scarecrow, observing the exchange in silence, steps forward. "We will move at your pace." He is calm and measured. "No one will be left behind."

The Cyborg turns toward the Scarecrow, studying him a moment. "You're…kind of, sort of, like me," he observes. "But you… You're in better shape with your mechanical parts."

The Scarecrow nods. "But I am incomplete, same as you, but I still function. Together, we can find what we need. I am sure of it. Logic is my compass, curiosity my fuel, and every mystery is a map to discovery."

The Cyborg let out a low, rasping chuckle. "Yeah… maybe."

***

Dotty, T.O.T.O., the Scarecrow, and their new companion continued down the forest path. The journey was slow, and the Cyborg's condition made it difficult to keep up.

As they walked, the Cyborg shared bits and pieces of its story. It had once been a guardian, tasked with protecting a settlement on the outskirts of the Citrusians' territory. But the settlement had fallen to the Tangarmarines long ago, and the Cyborg had been left behind, forgotten, and abandoned. Cyborg had wandered for years in the wilderness, scavenging for parts, trying to keep itself alive. But without a functioning energy core, its days were numbered.

"I do hope the light can help us," Dotty said quietly.

The Cyborg hesitated, then nodded. "It's… my last hope. If they don't have what I need… then I'm done for."

Dotty felt a knot of anxiety tighten in her chest. The light had become a symbol of salvation for all of them, the Scarecrow, and now the Cyborg. But the closer they got, the more she feared what they might find.

As the forest began to thin out, the light grew stronger, its glow piercing through the trees like the first rays of dawn. The air hummed with energy, and Dotty could feel a strange warmth radiating from the ground beneath her feet. They were close now. So close that she could almost touch the light.

But with that proximity came a growing sense of unease. The light was powerful. But it was also unpredictable, flickering and pulsing, which made Dotty's skin prickle.

Chapter 6

Sour and sweet

The orb, suspended by its complex network of cables and machinery, hung like a celestial body in the center of the clearing. Its surface crackled with the energy of yellow and green light that danced across it, illuminating the area with an ethereal glow.

The path leading to the orb was clear, a stark, yellow-dusted sand pathway that cut through the dense forest like a beacon. As they approached, the energy in the air intensified, the hair on Dotty's arms standing on end with the static charge.

"Look at that," Dotty whispered. The orb's presence was overwhelming, its power palpable in the charged air.

The Scarecrow, ever analytical, observed the orb with a critical eye. "That is remarkable," it stated, its voice barely audible over the hum of energy. "The engineering required to sustain such a structure must be advanced beyond anything I have seen."

The Cyborg, too, was captivated by the sight, his face reflecting the orb's vibrant light. "It's beautiful," it rasped, its usual harsh tone softened by awe. "I never imagined I'd see anything like this."

T.O.T.O barked softly, his sensors whirring as he took in the scene. Even the robotic dog seemed affected by the sheer magnitude of what they were witnessing.

As they stepped onto the yellowish sandy path, the ground beneath their feet vibrated gently, the rhythm syncing with the pulsations of the orb. Each step drew more energy from the surroundings, funneling it towards the orb at the path's end.

Dotty felt a pull towards the orb, an inexplicable force that beckoned them forward. With each step, the light grew brighter, the arcs of energy more frenetic. It was as if the orb was alive, aware of their approach and reacting to their presence.

"Be cautious," Dotty said, her voice tense as they walked. "We don't know what to expect when we reach the orb."

The Scarecrow nodded, its sensors constantly scanning the area for any signs of danger.

"The energy levels are increasing exponentially," it warned. "We must be prepared for instability."

Despite the Cyborg's deteriorated state, it is moving with a renewed sense of purpose. "If there's a chance that this orb can help me, then I'm willing to take the risk," it declared, its voice steady despite the crackle of static in the air. "It's funny, I never considered it a source that could help me. My creators put me on this planet years ago and never returned."

As they neared the orb, the pathway seemed to pulse more intensely. The yellow sand glows. The forest around them is behind them, exposing them to a vast clearing. The orb is looming and appears ever larger.

The orb, a massive, radiant sphere, pulsed with a light that was both blinding and enchanting. It hung mid-air, cradled by a network of vines that looked like veins, pulsing with luminescent life. This was no ordinary artifact; it was the lifeblood of the planet Citria, the source of its vitality and its consciousness.

As they stepped into the clearing, Dotty felt a surge of energy, a resonance that tingled through her bones. The air around the orb vibrated with power, filling the space with a hum that seemed to speak directly to their souls.

"Citria's heart," L.E.O. explained, his voice filled with reverence. "It's said that the Core was once a part of a celestial body that fell to this planet, forever changing its destiny. It's not just a source of energy but a beacon of wisdom. It holds the secrets of the universe in its continual pulse."

The group circled the orb cautiously, mesmerized by its beauty and the sheer force of its presence. Dotty reached out tentatively, her hand hovering near its surface. The air around it was warm, and an exhilarating energy shot jolted through her fingertips.

"It's more than I imagined," she whispered, turning to see Cyborg examining the orb's structure. "It feels alive, like it's aware of us."

Cyborg nodded, his sensors quietly whirring as they analyzed the orb. "Its structure is complex; beyond any technology we know. It's integrating organic and inorganic materials at a molecular level. I believe it could have the capability to communicate, through patterns in its pulsing."

Scarecrow, always seeking knowledge, pondered all of the implications.

"If we could understand its language, think of what we could learn! It might have knowledge stretching back to the origins of the universe."

As night deepened, they decided to set up camp in the clearing, under the watchful glow of the Citrus Core. The fire they built flickered in harmony with the orb's pulse, casting shadows that danced like spirits of the forest.

Sitting by the fire, Dotty felt a profound connection to everything around her. This journey, sparked by a crash and a series of unlikely events, had brought her to this extraordinary moment.

"This is our Citrus Oz," Dotty mused aloud, her voice thoughtful as her gaze lingered on the glowing orb. "A connectional story about the choices we make, the paths we stumble upon, and how we are bound to this place in ways we never imagined."

Her companions nodded, each of them lost in their thoughts.

***

The next morning, Scarecrow extended his arm, its sensors interacting with the energy field of the orb, trying to figure out how to get it to do something.

The Cyborg moved closer; its desperation evident. "What I want to know is, can it power me?" it asked, its voice a mixture of hope and urgency. "Can it give me the energy I need? I do not know how it works."

Before I could respond, the orb pulled brightly, a wave of energy rolling out in a visible shockwave. We braced ourselves, the force of the wave pushing against us like a strong wind.

When the energy subsided, I looked up, my gaze met the orb's vibrant surface. "I think it can do much more than that," I said, a spark of awe in my voice.

"Indeed, Dotty, you are right about that," Scarecrow replied.

***

The noise off in the distance grew louder. But in a nearby bush, leaves were shaking unnaturally.

My head snapped up to the noise in the sky, and then, close by, my gaze scanned the bushes. "Did you hear that? It sounds like a child crying."

Before anyone could respond, the air above them darkened with the silhouettes of dozens of small, winged creatures descending rapidly toward them. As we drew closer, their forms became clear—miniature Tangarmarines, bodies of sleek metal and aerodynamic, with wings that buzzed like those of oversized, hostile insects.

"These must be the Tangarmarine Flyers!" the Scarecrow analyzes, its voice calm despite the imminent threat. "They are scout units, designed for quick assaults."

The Cyborg shifts, positioning itself between me and the incoming swarm. "Get ready," it rasps.

I draw my laser cutter from my belt, my hand steady even as my heart pounds. T.O.T.O's sensors flicked to combat mode, emitting a low, defensive growl.

The Tangarmarine Flyers swarm in, their bodies glowing with a sinister orange light. They move with terrifying coordination, diving and swooping with metal razor-sharp talons extended. The first wave dives at me and my companions, their talons scratching against the Scarecrow's metal body with a screech of metal on metal.

I ducked as a flyer swooped at my head, feeling the air shift with its speed. I swung my laser cutter, catching the creature mid-dive. It shrieks as the laser sears through its wing, sending it spiraling to the ground.

"Keep them off the orb!" I shout. Realizing the creatures are not just attacking, but also converging on the orb and their small bodies bombarding cables and machinery. Its sharp limbs hacking at its delicate systems.

Scarecrow extends its arms, utilizing its built-in defensive mechanisms, a series of small, electrical discharges that zap at the Flyers. Each hit sends a Tangarmarine crashing to the ground, its body twitching and sparking from breaking apart.

Cyborg's rusted and failing body moved speed, its arms transforming into blasters that fire energy pulses. Each shot is precise, designed to incapacitate rather than destroy, as the Cyborg has no desire to cause more destruction than necessary.

T.O.T.O's jaws clamp onto a Tangarmarine, his mechanical strength crushes the creature's exoskeleton before he flings it aside.

The battle rages. The air fills with the sounds of buzzing wings, laser blasts, and the metallic clang of the Scarecrow's arms deflecting attacks. We fight back-to-back, under fire, a testament to the bonds we'd formed on our journey.

But the Tangarmarine Flyers were relentless. As one wave fell, another rose. I slash and dodge, my arms ache from the effort.

"We need to disrupt their coordination!" I yell over the chaos. "Scarecrow, can you send out an EMP pulse?"

The Scarecrow nods, its body already shifting to create the pulse. "Stand clear!" he warns, the lights on his body dimming momentarily before he unleashes a powerful electromagnetic pulse.

The effect was instantaneous. The air crackles with energy as the pulse sweeps through the clearing. The Tangarmarine Flyers, mid-flight, falter, their bodies seize up as the pulse overloads their systems. They drop like stones, crashing into the ground where they lie motionless.

I didn't waste a moment. "Now! While they're down!" I led the charge towards the orb, determined to protect it from further assault. The Cyborg and T.O.T.O covered me, ensuring no more Flyers could launch a surprise attack.

Reaching the orb, I inspect the damage. Some of the cables were nicked, and external circuits show signs of tampering. I set to work, my hands steady as I repair what I can, reinforcing the orb's defenses, only using my logic and sixth sense to fix it.

Scarecrow joins in, its sophisticated systems quickly diagnosing the more complex issues.

The clearing falls silent, the only sound is the gentle hum of the orb and heavy breaths..

A child appears suddenly before us, steps out of the bushes, and she's all dirty and wearing torn clothes. "You are heroic, I was so afraid they would hurt me. I am Mira. I was lost and separated from my family when the Flyers attacked us while we were gathering food supplies. I am from the city of Citria, You have saved me from them, thank you." Mira says as she wipes the tears from her face.

I wipe the sweat from my brow, turn to the Scarecrow and the Cyborg, and exchange knowing looks. "Well, thanks, I think it belongs to both of them. I couldn't have done it without them. Mira, we are going to the City. We will take you there; it's better in numbers anyway."

Mira runs over to me and hugs me tightly, her little arms pressing around my waist.

The Cyborg nods and smiles slightly with the exchange, its eyes dimming with fatigue. "We protect each other, right, Dotty?" he says. "That's what heroes do."

"Indeed. Well, it looks as if the Orb is okay for now. I know nothing of its power or how it can help us, but I think if we can reach the city, someone can help us, surely." I say.

Cyborg looks at the Orb, trying to decipher if he can find a way to repair himself with it. " I am unsure what to do or how to use it. Perhaps if we go to the City, I can ask them."

"I think that is a good idea, we need help. What do you think, Scarecrow?" Dotty turned to face him.

"I believe you are correct. I do not know myself, as I was never taught to fix or use it." Scarecrow stated as he looked up at the Orb.

Mira steps between us, "They can help in the City. My father works with the mayor on top-secret things. If anyone can repair you, they can."

"Then it's settled. But first, we needed food and to rest for the night, as we were not close enough to walk to it today." Dotty remarked on the obvious.

Chapter 7

A Luminary Electronic Overseer

Dotty and her companions, fatigued and battered, trudged along the periphery of the dense forest that bordered the Citrusian city. The light from the Orb had dimmed, signaling the closure of the city's gates.

They searched for a place to rest. There were moments when Dotty found herself staring at the Cyborg.

She was completely caught off guard by its unexpected human quirks, moments when it attempted humor or shared snippets of its past. He revealed that human emotions lingered within its circuitry. These glimpses into the Cyborg's lingering human side and valor to protect them made Dotty appreciate him.

They moved deeper into the forest, and a faint glow caught Dotty's eye. "Over there," she pointed towards a clearing where soft light emanated from a grove of luminescent trees. The group headed towards the light, hoping to find somewhere safe to rest.

The clearing was serene. The air was filled with a gentle hum of bioluminescent lemon and lime citrus plants that cast a soothing light around them. In the center of this natural alcove, a large, hollowed-out tree offered a perfect refuge. They approached cautiously, mindful of any potential dangers that might lurk within.

As they approached the tree, a shimmering figure materialized before them.

A holographic projection that flickered with every move. The lion's mane rippled with a rainbow spectrum of colors, its holographic form translucent, the image stuttering as if it were struggling to maintain coherence.

"Who goes there?" The lion's voice crackled through the air, more curious than threatening.

"I'm Dotty, and these are my friends," Dotty introduced, gesturing to T.O.T.O, Mira, the Scarecrow, and Cyborg. "We mean you no harm. We're just looking for a place to rest for the night."

The holographic lion studied them, its form stabilizing slightly as it processed her words. "You may find shelter here," it said finally, its tone resigned. "I am L.E.O., once the guardian of this grove. I am the Luminary Electronic Overseer. But I fear I offer little protection now."

Dotty noted the sadness in the lion's voice and expression. "What happened to you, L.E.O.?" she asked gently.

"Before I lost my data, I was not just any guardian. I was also the grove's luminary entertainer. I was programmed not only to protect but to keep morale high. My programming included an extensive library of jokes, songs, and dramatic tales. All performed with holographic enhancements to dazzle my audience.

I was famous for "Monday Night Howls," a weekly event, recounting heroic tales from Citrusian history, interspersed with light shows and what he liked to call "roar-along" songs. These events attracted Citrusians from all corners of the region.

One of my favorite jokes went like this:

"Why doesn't secrecy last long in the forest? Because the trees will eventually spill the beans... or should I say, the seeds!"

Dotty and Cyborg looked at each other and then back at the lion.

Scarecrow raised one of his rusty eyebrows, "Is that meant to be funny, lion? My logic doesn't compute it."

Mira, who had been playing with T.O.T.O., giggled.

L.E.O's form flickered, a ghost of a roar escaping him before fading into a sigh. "Yes, well, I was designed to be brave mostly, the protector of the Citrusian outskirts. But during a data wipe, an attack by the Tangamarines, I lost much of my programming. My courage… my essence. Now, I am but a shadow of what I once was."

Dotty looked at the lion, "I am so sorry that happened to you."

The group settled into the tree's shelter. The Scarecrow was positioned near the entrance, while T.O.T.O. curled beside Dotty.

"You still seem very brave to me, being here despite everything," Dotty offered, thinking out loud, trying to reassure the holographic lion.

L.E.O's mane dimmed with his chuckle. "Perhaps. But without my full data, I am incomplete. I fear I am no longer the guardian I once was."

As night deepened, the Scarecrow and Dotty worked on minor repairs and system checks, ensuring everyone was at least in working condition. Meanwhile, L.E.O recounted tales of the past of what he could remember, battles he had fought, and the peace that once reigned over the grove.

The Cyborg, listening intently, finally spoke up. "Isn't there a way to restore your data, L.E.O.? To bring back your courage and humor data?"

L.E.O's face brightened for a moment. "There might be a way. Deep within the Citrusian city, is a databank, a repository of all knowledge and history. If I could access it, I could restore what I've lost."

Dotty considered this. "When we get into the city, we could try to help you regain your data. We'll be looking for answers and assistance ourselves. Together, we can find a way."

L.E.O looked at her, his digital face conveying gratitude. "That would mean a great deal to me. To be whole again, to truly protect. To make everyone laugh..."

***

As twilight painted the forest in shades of purple, yellow, and gold, they found themselves by a small, glowing river, its waters reflecting the bioluminescent plants lining its banks. They decided to camp for the night. As the Cyborg built a fire, a skill he had learned and adapted to despite some of his more predominant mechanical natures, I foraged close by.

Returning with a handful of edible fruits, I found the Cyborg staring intently at the fire, his face illuminated by the flickering light. Scarecrow, T.O.T.O., L.E.O., and the young child slept early without eating from the exhausting day. I could see it was taking its toll on everyone, including myself.

Dotty sat next to the Cyborg. She offered him some fruit, and surprisingly, he took it and began to eat it. Dotty notices that one of his hands is not metal. For a moment, they sat in silence and enjoyed the presence of the forest by the warmth of the fire.

"It's strange," she began, breaking the silence, "how moments like these can feel so serene, even when I'm far from everything familiar."

The Cyborg turned to look at her, his eye reflecting the firelight. "Yes, it is. But.. " he said thoughtfully, "it's not the place that makes us feel at ease, but more so, the company we keep."

Surprised by his response, Dotty smiled. She is thinking about his comments, which blur the lines between man and machine in him. Revealing the depth of his character, Cyborg possesses.

Cyborg ventures off and discovers a little river a short distance away, with illuminated winged creatures lighting up the darkness.

Cyborg reaches out his human hand to Dotty, leaning against a tree, lost in thought. "Come with me," he says.

Dotty looks at him, "Where are we going?"

"Trust me."

He takes her to the spot. Dotty believes this place is magical. The river sparkles with the winged creatures dipping and weaving in and out of the space.

"This is so beautiful, thank you for bringing me here. Do you think it's okay to wash up here?"

I believe so, I drank some of it earlier. Although my functions aren't working properly, I did not detect any toxins. It is full of nutrients for human consumption." Cyborg knelt at the river and began washing his arms and face.

"Good enough for me. I am glad to be able to clean up. Do you mind if I get out of these clothes? It's dark enough here." Dotty looked at Cyborg as she removed her clothing.

Cyborg didn't have to reply, Dotty was already naked and walking into the river. Her silhouette made Cyborg stop what he was doing and freeze to stare at her body disappearing into the water.

Dotty, smiling, waves him in. "Come in, it's warm!"

Cyborg, removing only his shirt, walks in with his pants intact.

Dotty observes his chiseled chest and muscles; his face and hair are clean from the water. He reveals more of his masculine human features. Wet, he reaches to wipe his hair from his face, the wings on his back expanding, showing his wide, muscled back.

Dotty couldn't help but stare, attracted to him. She shook it off and turned her back on him to clean herself. Turning back, catching Cyborg staring as she moves, showing her perky breasts above the water. The light of the creatures cascades light on all the right parts as she leaves the water.

Cyborg takes his time to leave the water, revealing his pants clinging to his wide thighs and ample buttocks. Dotty is surprised by his engorged manhood. If it were daylight, she would be showing that she was blushing.

Later that night, as Dotty lay by the fire to sleep, the Cyborg made them, she rekindled her thoughts of the night:

Something about the quiet moment together, the easy silence filled with the sounds of the flickering flames and the distant nocturnal calls of the forest, makes Dotty aware of my growing fondness for him. She watches how the firelight dances across his partially metallic features, softened, making him seem like a whole human.

As we sat there, sharing food and the silent understanding, Dotty couldn't help but feel that, despite his partial synthetic origins, there was a genuine connection, something more profound growing between us.

***

While making their way through a particularly dense part of the forest the next day, a sudden storm forced them to seek shelter under a large, leafy canopy. The rain poured around them, creating a water curtain that shielded them in privacy. I slipped on the wet undergrowth. Our eyes met for half a heartbeat, and the world outside the canopy disappeared. The rain muffled the sounds of the forest. My heart raced, not from the fall, but from the closeness of the Cyborg, whose gaze held mine with an intensity that spoke of more, something unsaid.

"Thank you," I whisper, my voice barely audible over the rain. He sets me down, but I grab his hand in mine briefly. I feel the skin of his fingers, there is warmth.

"You're welcome," the Cyborg replies, his voice low. Slowly, he released my hand from his, but the space between us felt charged.

Chapter 8

Bitter greetings

As the first rays of dawn stretch across the forest, painting the world in hues of gold and green, my companions and I prepare to leave the shelter of the grove. They have promised the young Citrusian child, Mira, that they would help her return to her family within the walls of the Citrusian city. Spirits were high with the prospect of entering the city. But not only to reunite Mira with her family. To find the resources they needed for their quests.

However, upon arriving at the towering gates of the city, they found them firmly shut, the massive doors sealed without any indication of opening soon. The group was puzzled and slightly dismayed, having assumed that the city gates would open with the morning light.

I approached the gate and knocked loudly, her fists echoing against the sturdy metal. "Hello! We need to enter. We have a child here, Mira, who belongs inside with her family!" I call out.

Minutes tick by with no response, the gate is impassive as ever.

Just as I am about to knock again, a small panel slides open, and a pair of bright green eyes peer out at us.

"What's your business?" the gatekeeper's voice is gruff. His skin, a leathery, withered rind of dark green. His vocals filter through the metal barrier.

I explain our situation and introduce each member of the group.

The gatekeeper scrutinizes them, his gaze lingers on L.E.O.'s flickering form and the Cyborg's rusted exterior. "The child can enter, but the rest of you... What can you offer the city in exchange for entry? Resources are tight, and we can't just open our gates for everyone."

I exchanged a worried glance with the others. We hadn't anticipated this.

Scarecrow speaks up first. "I know advanced agriculture and soil rejuvenation techniques. I can share this with your farmers to enhance your crop yields."

L.E.O adds, "And I can provide entertainment and historical archives once I regain access to my full functions. I can boost morale and offer education through my narratives."

The Cyborg, looking worse for wear, had its own valuable offer to give: "I have experience in defense systems. I can help fortify your city, work on your security protocols."

The gatekeeper considers their offers for a moment, his face unreadable. Finally, he agrees. "Alright, you may enter, but we'll need to see immediate contributions from each of you. The city doesn't tolerate freeloaders."

I thanked him, relief washing over me as the gates slowly creaked open. They usher Mira through first, and she runs off ahead eagerly, excited to be home, quickly waving goodbye to us. As we enter, I feel safe here, but I am still carrying the weight of our promises, this weight on my shoulders. We all need to make good on our word, not just for my sake, but to help restore Leo and assist the Cyborg in finding a new energy core.

****

The Citrusians are a unique species native to Citria, distinguished by their vibrant, citrus-like bodies. These beings are an extraordinary sight, with skin that resembles the rind of various citrus fruits, oranges, lemons, limes, and grapefruits, giving them a colorful and textured appearance. The hues of their skin are not just for show; they also indicate their roles and statuses within Citrusian society, with brighter, more vivid colors often signifying higher social standing or particular aptitudes.

Citrusians are known for their refreshing lemony scent, a natural byproduct of the citrus oils that permeate their skin. This scent serves a dual purpose: it acts as a natural deterrent against some of the planet's more aggressive fauna, and that of the Tangarmarines.

Their diet is primarily based on a practice they call 'stellar sipping,' where they absorb and photosynthesize sunlight, much like plants on Earth. However, they supplement this with a diet of the planet's rich flora, particularly the abundant varieties of nectar and citrus-producing plants. This diet is necessary for their physical nourishment but also plays a crucial role in maintaining the vibrant color of their citrus-like skin. The brighter the skin, the more radiant and beautiful you are deemed.

***

The streets were bustling with Citrusians going about their day. The contrast between life inside the walls and the quiet, sometimes harsh world outside was stark. As they made their way through the city, the group attracted curious glances, outsiders were a rarity.

Their first stop was the agricultural sector, where the Scarecrow immediately began consulting with the local farmers, sharing knowledge, and demonstrating techniques that drew interested and appreciative crowds.

Cyborg worked alongside the city's engineers, his expertise proving invaluable as they assessed and upgraded security measures, ensuring the city was better protected against potential threats

By the time they had reunited to check on Mira, the child was safely back in the arms of her grateful family, who thanked Dotty and her group profusely.

Walking through the bustling streets of the Citrusian city, Dotty and her companions absorbed the vibrant culture around them. The City was a hub of activity, with vendors selling exotic fruits and shouting prices of goods. Artisans were showing off their intricate crafts as they walked by.

L.E.O. walked on and continued to do what he did best, entertain and educate, even as they searched for help for the Scarecrow and the Cyborg.

As they approached the city's technological district, L.E.O's form flickered with a brighter light, signaling his attempt to lift the mood. "Ah, I recall a joke," L.E.O. started, his voice gaining a theatrical lilt. "Why did the robot apply for a job in the garden?"

The group glanced at each other, amused curiosity on their faces. Dotty, playing along, shrugged. "Okay, why?"

L.E.O.'s holographic face beamed as if he were smiling. "Because he wanted to sprout a few new connections!" His laugh, a digitized approximation, filled the air around them.

The Scarecrow, ever the practical one, responded with a dry, "I suppose networking is important in all fields."

Even the Cyborgs demeanor, usually quite serious, emitted a low chuckle at the sound, more of a static buzz than laughter. "That's... quite funny, L.E.O."

Their first stop was a center known for advanced robotics and AI, exactly the place that might hold the key to upgrading the Scarecrow's intelligence and finding a new energy core for the Cyborg.

Inside the center, they were greeted by a team of engineers and the scientists were intrigued.

The Scarecrow immediately engaged with a specialist in agricultural robotics, discussing potential enhancements and software upgrades that could elevate his ability to analyze and manage soil health and crop cycles more efficiently.

Meanwhile, Dotty and Cyborg spoke with an expert in energy systems, explaining Cyborg's dire need for a new core. The expert examined him, carefully nodding along as he listened to the descriptions of his current system's specifications and failures.

"We can certainly help," the engineer finally declared, tapping away at a tablet. "We've developed a range of high-efficiency cores that can be compatible with older models. We'll need to run some diagnostics first, but I'm confident we can restore you to full operation."

The Cyborg's single metal eye lit up, a rare show of emotion from part machine. "Thank you. That's more than I've dared hope for in a long time."

The technicians took the Scarecrow and Cyborg away for detailed assessments and repairs, and Dotty and L.E.O. found themselves with a moment to rest. They sat on a nearby bench, watching the city life swirl around them.

"You did a great job back there, L.E.O.," Dotty said, watching the lion's colors gently shift. "And not just with the joke. You've been a big help."

L.E.O's projection flickered warmly. "I'm just glad to be of use again. It feels... good to be involved, and share what I know, and I can still do."

Dotty nodded. "Once we get the full database restored, I think you'll be doing a lot more than just telling jokes and your courage back."

L.E.O looked thoughtful, his digital form casting colorful reflections on the smooth surface of the bench. "I look forward to that. And I'll find some new jokes to add to my collection."

Dotty laughed. "Sounds good to me."

Chapter 9

The threat

The city, vibrant and bustling with the harmonious chaos of daily life, suddenly fell into an eerie silence. The atmosphere thickened, charged with a palpable tension that heralded the arrival of something, or someone, *ominous*.

In the heart of the City, a chilling wind began to blow, swirling with an unnatural force. It swept through the streets, carrying a faint, whispering voice that seemed to echo from the shadows. The citizens of the City stopped in their tracks, their faces turning towards the city's main gate with a mix of fear and anticipation. T.O.T.O. L.E.O., the Scarecrow, the newly energized Cyborg, and I gather together, sensing the imminent threat.

As we make our way towards the source of the disturbance, the ground beneath our feet trembles slightly, and the sky darkens, as if the sun itself were cowering from what was to come. At the city's main gate, the crowd parts to reveal a figure shrouded in a flowing black cloak, her presence emanating malevolence that chills the very air.

The Sorceress.

Her eyes are glowing a fierce crimson red, like a blood orange. She scans the crowd until it lands on me and my group. With a sinister smile, she raised her hands, and the gates slammed shut behind her with a thunderous crash that echoed through the city streets. She begins to walk forward, each step resonant with power, her voice amplifying as she speaks.

"Citizens of this forsaken city," the Sorceress begins, her voice, a mesmerizing blend of charm and venom. "I have come for what is rightfully mine. The power of the Orb. You have kept it from me for too long by your futile protections."

The crowd murmurs in fear, their expressions darting anxiously among themselves. I step forward; my expression resolute. "The orb isn't yours to take. It belongs to everyone."

The Sorceress's laugh was cold, echoing off the city walls. "Naive girl, do you think you can stop me? You, who are stumbling into a war that predates your existence in this world!"

L.E.O's holographic mane flaring with intensity, speaks next. "She is not stumbling alone, Sorceress. We stand with her, and together, we have fortified this city against your darkness."

Unfazed, the Sorceress glances dismissively at L.E.O. "A broken hologram and his band of misfits," she laughs. "You will not deter me from getting what I want, and I'll take your little dog too, when this is over."

With a swift motion, she casts a spell that sends a pulse of dark energy rippling through the streets. Windows shatter, and the ground cracks, but the city's defenses, bolstered by the Cyborg's recent enhancements, hold strong and let the Sorceress' magic dissipate.

"Impressive," she admits begrudgingly. "But not invincible." Her gaze fixes on Dotty. "You are the heart of this resistance. Tell me, child, why do you fight so hard for a world that isn't yours?"

I meet her gaze, unflinching. "Because it's the right thing to do. Because power like this," I gesture to the orb, visible in the distance, glowing steadily, "shouldn't be used to harm or control. It should protect, give life, not take it."

The Sorceress studies Dotty for a long moment, her expression unreadable. Then, without warning, she unleashes another wave of dark energy, more focused this time, directed solely at Dotty.

Reacting quickly, the Scarecrow steps in, absorbing the brunt of the attack with its own body. Its circuits crackling with the overflow of dark magic. "Your fight is not with her alone," the Scarecrow intones, its voice distorted but firm.

The Sorceress recoils slightly; her attack thwarted. "Very well," she says, her tone dripping with malice and hatred. "If it is a fight you want, it is a fight you will get. But know this—you will not win. The Tangarmarine army is already on its way, and with its numbers, not even your precious orb will save you. And Dotty," the Sorceress pauses, "your interests are not pure, though, are they? You wish to return home. That is the real reason you interfere with these matters. I can take you home right now if you say it. Just say the word, girl, and I'll grant it… No?... I will let you think it over."

The Sorceress vanishes, her departure leaving a vacuum of silence in its wake.

The city is left in a state of heightened alert, the citizens rally around me and my friends. The mayor of the City has a determined and serious look on his face. "You have done much for us, strangers," he says. "But you have threatened our very existence. We must prepare for what is to come."

He pauses, looking each of them in the eye. His gaze lingered on Dotty. "The Sorceress must be destroyed," he declares with a firmness that contains no argument. "As long as she remains a threat, our world will never be safe. You have asked for our help to restore your friends and to find a way home for you, Dotty. We are willing to fulfill these wishes, under one condition."

The group exchanges uneasy glances, and the weight of the mayor's words hangs heavily in the air. I stepped forward, my resolve hardening. "What condition?" I ask, my voice steady despite my fear.

The mayor moved uncomfortably. The seriousness of the situation was reflected in his tone. "You must lead the charge to eliminate the Sorceress. With your unique skills, the bonds you have formed with each other, you have a chance to succeed where others might fail. If you agree, we will provide everything necessary for your journey and subsequent needs, resources, information, and support to ensure your success and safe return home."

The proposal struck me like a physical blow. The thought of leading a direct attack against such a powerful adversary was daunting, but the stakes were higher than ever. It's my chance to return home. The lives of countless innocent people rested on this decision.

L.E.O.'s form, shimmering slightly with the strain of his incomplete data, speaks up, his voice shaky. "We came together under extraordinary circumstances. This is no different. We will face it together, just as we have faced everything so far as one."

***

The Scarecrow, with its newly upgraded intelligence, says, "The tactical advantage lies in striking decisively and using our combined strengths. The Sorceress may not expect such a bold move."

The Cyborg cleaned and its metal parts polished, with more of its systems humming softly, closed its eyes briefly in assent. "I am ready to continue fighting, not just for survival but for the peace of this planet; this is my battle for my home."

I took a deep breath, looking around at my friends, each ready to stand with me. I thought it over, I knew what I must do.

I nodded firmly; I made my decision. "We'll do it, and I will fight with you. We'll stop the Sorceress. For the city, its people, and the peace of this world. And yes, so that I can go home."

The mayor's expression softened; relief mingled with resolve passed across his features. "Then let us prepare," he said, turning, signaling several of his aides. "You will have all the support Citria can offer. Together, we will ensure the end of the Sorceress's reign of terror."

As plans were hastily drawn and resources marshaled, my companions and I went to engineering for further upgrades and planning.

Chapter 10

T.O.T.O, Scarecrow, Cyborg, L.E.O,

Oh my!

The engineers frantically worked for weeks before the battle, with the team's main focus on repairing Dotty's friends.

They made sure every member, including T.O.T.O., is in peak condition. Inside a well-lit workshop bustling with activity, engineers and technicians moved with purpose, and their expertise was directed at enhancing and repairing their robotic canine companion.

One engineer focused on upgrading T.O.T.O.'s integrated laser system. Installing a new focusing lens would allow greater control over the beam's intensity and width. This enhancement was designed to switch between a wide beam for close-range encounters.

The engineer monitored his computer and then informed Scarecrow of his upgrades. "You have received significant upgrades to ensure it can play a crucial role in defense. Engineers and technicians worked meticulously to enhance their capabilities, transforming it from a simple, intelligent field guardian into a formidable combat asset. Here's a detailed look at the key upgrades to improve your decision-making and strategic planning abilities. In other words, your brain, if you will. You are equipped with a new, state-of-the-art processor. This upgrade significantly boosted its analytical skills, allowing it to process vast amounts of data in real-time, making it an effective strategist on the battlefield.

Understanding the physical demands of combat, we are reinforcing your exoskeleton with lightweight, high-strength composite materials. This increased its durability and flexibility, allowing it to move swiftly and withstand direct hits from enemy fire. Also, you're outfitted with a variety of integrated weapons systems."

Another engineer working on him explained more about his upgrades to the group gathered around them. "A Tactical Communication Array is a new communication array that allows Scarecrow to maintain constant contact with the city's defense network. It coordinates with other units and relays vital information about enemy movements and tactics. This system was encrypted to prevent interception by enemy forces.

A Self-Repair Mechanism is one of the most critical upgrades, a self-repair mechanism. Utilizing nanotechnology, this system could quickly address any damage the Scarecrow might sustain in combat, from minor circuitry faults to more significant structural issues, thereby keeping it operational longer under harsh conditions.

We have advanced Scarecrow's mobility with hydraulic leg actuators and anti-gravity modules. This allows for rapid movements across varied terrains, from leaping over obstacles to quick bursts of speed, giving it a tactical advantage in maneuvering during skirmishes.

With these comprehensive upgrades, Scarecrow is transformed from a humble agricultural protector into a key asset in the city's defense strategy."

"What do you think?" The scarecrow spun to show the others his gleaming new metal accessories.

I believe that with you on our side, we will win this war! L.E.O. roared.

"Agreed. There will be no match for us!" Cyborg smiled, "My upgrades are substantial as well. My failing energy core was replaced with a new, high-capacity core designed for intense combat scenarios, which gave vitality to my human body. This new core increased my operational time and provides a much-needed boost to all my systems. This allows quicker responses and more sustained activity without the risk of power failure, renewing its stamina and endurance. My tactical artificial intelligence is upgraded with the latest battlefield management software, providing me with real-time data on enemy movements and battlefield conditions. Plus, this AI chip embedded into the eye will also assist in making strategic decisions quickly.

"Impressive," L.E.O. responded. "My holographic projection received a significant upgrade, too, increasing the clarity and range of my imagery. This enhancement allows me to appear more lifelike and project multiple images simultaneously, creating decoys to confuse the enemy."

Dotty looked at everyone as she entered the room, "You are all so stunning. This is the most impressive room of technology advancement I have ever seen."

With everyone's upgrades complete, L.E.O. and Cyborg joined a meeting with the city's defense commanders. L.E.O's form flickered slightly as he adjusted to his enhanced projection capabilities. The room was filled with tactical displays and the low murmur of voices discussing last-minute preparations.

"L.E.O., how do you feel about the upgrades?" One of the engineers asked, a note of light in his tone amidst the gravity of their situation.

"Quite invigorating!" L.E.O. responded, his voice booming around the room. "I feel like a brand-new lion. I'm positively *electrifying* now!" He paused, a simulated smile playing across his holographic lips.

There was a brief silence before the room erupted into laughter, groans, and chuckles.

Despite the tension, L.E.O.'s dad joke lightens the atmosphere, a reminder of his original role in lifting spirits.

"Always good to keep morale high, L.E.O.," a commander commented, shaking her head with a smile.

"Yes, indeed," L.E.O. continued, his tone turning serious. "But let us not forget the task at hand. I am here to assist in any way I can. The enemy may not appreciate my humor, but they will certainly come to respect our resolve."

"Remember," L.E.O. called out as they left, "stay charged and ready. Today, we fight not just for Citria, but for the future!"

"I couldn't have worded it better myself, L.E.O.," looking at Dotty.

T.O.T.O., Cyborg, Dotty, L.E.O., and Scarecrow stood and looked out onto the battle-fields, their new armor shining in the sunset.

Tomorrow would be a day they remember.

Chapter 11

Her Citrus is sweet

As the night before the battle with the Tangarmarines enveloped Citria in darkness, Dotty and Cyborg found themselves finalizing their plans under the light of the four moons. They were huddled in a makeshift command tent, surrounded by maps and digital displays, each highlighting the strategic points around the city where the Tangarmarines were likely to attack.

The tactical tent was quiet, save from the occasional rustle of maps or the soft beeping of the equipment. T.O.T.O lay underneath the table, resting.

They were focused on their tasks, but an undercurrent of tension and emotions, rather than strategic, pulsed between them.

Dotty, marking a critical pathway on the map, glanced up at Cyborg, catching him staring at her with an intensity that made her pause. She put down the marker and met his gaze.

She took in all of him. Making a note of the muscles that stretched over parts of his shirt. His biceps and broad shoulders looked healthy, his skin was tan and clean. Something erotic stirred inside her.

The rest of the group left early, saying they needed to be well-rested before the battle. However, Cyborg, experiencing heightened emotions, stayed to see if they were missing anything.

"Are you okay?" she asked, her voice low, trying to shake off the feelings she was having.

He hesitated, his mechanical parts whirring softly as if adjusting to more than just tactical data. "I am… concerned," he finally said, his voice betraying a hint of vulnerability. "Not just for the battle, but for us, for what might happen tomorrow."

Dotty felt a tightness in her chest, understanding immediately what he meant.

The future was uncertain.

She stepped closer, her resolve firming. "I know," she replied, softly touching his arm. "I'm scared, too. Not just of losing the fight, but of losing… this. What we've found together."

Cyborg extended his hand, a human gesture, and Dotty took it, her fingers intertwining with his metallic ones. The contrast between human warmth and the coolness of metal seemed to encapsulate the essence of their relationship, different yet somehow connected.

"We have faced a few challenges now," he said, his tone more confident as he spoke. "We have learned from each other, and I think we have grown together. Whatever happens tomorrow, I want you to know that... you have changed me. For the better."

Dotty squeezed his hand. "And you have changed me, too," she admitted. "I don't know what the future holds, but I'm glad that whatever time we have, we're spending it together."

They stood in silence for a moment, the noise of the preparations outside fading out. Finally, Dotty spoke up, her voice steady despite her emotions. "Let's make sure we fight not just for survival, but for a future. A future where we can explore what this,.." she gestured between them, "..can become."

Nodding, Cyborg released her hand and gently pressed closer, his hand moving on the small side of her back. She was so close; she could feel his heat. He gave in to his desire briefly, kissing her cheek, then let go, holding back.

He turned back to face the map. "Then let's plan to win this battle," he said, his voice laced with determination.

They walked back to their separate quarters to rest just before dawn; the silent promise hung between them.

Cyborg stopped, turning around from where he came and walking toward her. Standing there, he grasped her face gently with both hands, "I will help you go home; I promise you this."

"But, what if I said that I am not in such a hurry to leave you?" Dotty's eyes filled with tears.

He looked intently at her and studied her features, his thumb rubbing her cheeks gently. "I will go wherever you go, my lady."

Dotty took a deep breath, feeling the sincerity, letting it resonate within her. "And what if *'wherever'* means staying here, on Citria?" she asked, the possibility hanging between them like a fragile thread. "What if you could leave here, would you?"

He paused, his mechanical heart processing the weight of her question. After a moment, he replied, "Dotty, when I was sitting abandoned in that forest, I felt I was but a machine. I followed programming without question. But now, with every upgrade, every improvement, my heart is beating for you, and I've become something more. I feel things. You've taught me about choice, about desire. I can thrive on any planet if you're in it."

His words brought a small, hopeful smile to Dotty's face. "And if I choose to try the portal? To see if it will truly take me home. Would you risk it all and follow me there?"

"Yes. I would follow to the ends of the earth," Cyborg confirmed it without hesitation, by embracing her in the darkness. "Wherever the journey leads, whatever risks it involves, I'm with you. How could I not want to see more, especially if it's by your side?"

He was so different, yet so perfectly aligned with her. "Then let's promise, no matter what happens, we'll face it together. Whether here on Citria or somewhere across the universe."

"Together," he echoed, his one digital eye and one human eye locking with hers, a vow made not just in words but in the silent language of shared souls. He took her in his arms and kissed her gently on the lips. Dotty melted from the heat of his skin. A fire lit within, and she kissed him harder. Her breasts firmly pressed against his chest, Dotty's breath quickened as the cool metal of his synthetic hand traced the curve of her jaw, a contrast against the warmth radiating from his human palm. His one digital eye pulsed with a soft blue glow, while his human eye burned with something raw, something achingly real. Passion.

"Together," he whispered again, and the word was not just a promise. It was a plea, a surrender.

Dotty leaned in, their lips meeting in a kiss that began as a whisper, a soft brush of warmth that sent a shiver down her spine. Her fingers traced the sharp lines of his jaw, feeling the smooth, cool metal on one side of his face. It was a striking contrast to his heated skin beneath the living half of his body. She ran her hands through his hair, pressing against him with the softness of her curves, and she gasped as an electric thrill from him ran through her.

Her heart pounded wildly beneath her skin. He tasted like a cool summer breeze on a hot night, and she craved him. Dotty's hands roamed, feeling the juxtaposition of metal and muscle, her touch a map tracing where metal met skin.

Her voice trembled with a mix of excitement and vulnerability. "I've never..." discovering with her hand, finding the hardened truth of how badly he wanted her."

"I know," he murmured, his voice a soothing blend of static and human warmth. "I am still human where it matters most."

His touch was both delicate and possessive. His left hand, which had metal fingers, slid beneath the fabric of her clothing. His cool touch on her hard nipples made her gasp. Her body moved instinctively, as their mouths collided with growing hunger. Their tongues explored with feverish need, her fingers threading through his hair, tugging him closer as if she could pull him into her skin. His hand slid along her thigh, lifting her leg to wrap around his hip, letting her feel the undeniable evidence of how much he craved her and just how deeply he was already hers. They moved together, caught in a heat that blurred the world beyond their breath and touch.

His human hand slipped beneath her shirt, tracing the curve of her waist, then higher, fingers brushing her bare skin and sending shivers. Dotty's breath quickened. Her own hands under his shirt roamed to his chest, savoring the contrast between the warmth of living flesh and the cold precision of metal. His hand slid lower, past her navel, down the curve of her hip, and found the heat of her, the place where all her longing burned hottest.

"I promise to be gentle," he growled.

"Don't you dare," Dotty whispered, grabbing his groin and rubbing it through his trousers, initiating another grunt from him.

"Yes, but only at first." He moaned softly in her ear.

His metallic fingers, already under her shirt, gliding upward, over her ribs, until his palm cradled the curve of her breast.

Her hands traced the hard ridges of his abdomen, exploring with curiosity.

T.O.T.O barked at an alien-looking rodent scurrying by, and both jumped. Suddenly, coming to their senses and aware of their surroundings, they stopped and adjusted their clothing.

"Perhaps we should take this elsewhere," Dotty panted.

Cyborg pulled her close, "I think I should just go to bed. We have a big day tomorrow. I am not sure if I am capable of being gentle. I wouldn't want to hurt you. Besides, I would have to ravage you until you're screaming."

"But that's why I want you tonight, in case one of us doesn't make it out of this. She smiled and bit her bottom lip. "Plus, I want you to make me scream." She couldn't help but press her body against him again, her desire building with every heartbeat. She pulled him in the direction of her tent. It didn't take much convincing; he followed her, squeezing her buttocks.

"Show me," she whispered in the tent, challenging him. She undressed to reveal her naked and perfect body on display for him to look upon. She stepped closer, fingers trembling slightly as she began to undress him.

In that moment, his mind flickered back to the first time he saw her in the water, how desperately he'd wanted to feel every inch of her.

"Are you sure about this?" Cyborg's voice was low, almost a whisper. "The machine inside me mixed with my human side... It's powerful. I don't know if I can hold back, and I want you to know, it is nothing you have ever experienced."

Dotty's eyes locked onto his. "Don't make me ask twice. I want you—right now." Touching herself, drawing him in.

"Mm, but maybe I want you to beg," he threw his shirt over his head, taking it off, and revealed a perfectly muscled chest. Only one breast plate over his heart was metal and a few wires that disappeared on his skin, the rest was human to the touch.

"Please." She begged, smiling at him.

He guided her to the makeshift bed on the floor. Two bodies, a perfect contrast and mix of flesh and metal harmony in the darkness..

"You're the most beautiful thing I've ever seen," he said softly, his eyes tracing the curves of her naked body, legs parted, silently inviting him in.

"I want you." She moaned, her fingers dancing over her entrance.

His breath hitched as he watched her, dark desire burning in his eyes. "Mm, you're mine," he growled, voice low and possessive. He entered with agonizing slowness, every inch claiming her, grounding her in the reality of his touch. His lips found her nipples. He took them in his mouth one at a time, paying attention to ignite her senses and desire. Dotty gasped, the sheer intensity of his heat and strength, overwhelming her. Cyborg's electric waves of pleasure surged through her, setting her senses alight. She was his, completely and without question.

Entwined and moving together, they dissolved into each other's soft moans, fevered kisses. She pushed against him, and he answered in kind. Overcome with ecstasy, they climaxed together, intense and overwhelming. Dotty's legs trembled, her breath coming in sharp, shallow bursts.

For a moment, there was only stillness.

Sweaty and trembling, Dotty looked up into his mismatched eyes, her pulse still racing, and saw her longing mirrored back at her.

In the dim glow of the room, skin against skin, Dotty clung to him. Her head lay against his chest, the rise and fall of his breathing beneath her ear, the quiet hum of his mechanical heart steady and real. In that moment, there was no war, no orb, no unknown tomorrow, only this, only them.

"Together," she whispered, a breath of a promise wrapped in aching need.

He pulled her close, holding her like the world might slip away.

Then, slowly, she slid her body on top of him, already hungry again, aching to feel him once more. This time slower, deeper.

A second dance of heat and light in the shadows of a broken world, where nothing existed but them, and no part of her wanted it to end.

Chapter 12

The Tangarmarines

An oppressive silence dawned over the Citrusian city. Dark clouds rolled across the sky, casting a pall over the sunlit orchards and vibrant markets that had, until recently, been bustling with life.

We awoke with little sleep between us, hearing the commotion outside, still entangled in each other's arms.

"This is it. Let's kick some alien butt so we can finally start our life together!" Cyborg said as he kissed my forehead before getting up to get dressed.

I yawned and tapped his bare ass as he turned his backside to me. "Just don't die, I need more nights like last night."

"You mean early mornings," he chuckled, getting changed.

***

The City's citizens, over the last week, have fortified their homes and taken shelter. They watched anxiously as my companions prepared for the impending battle. The air was thick with tension, the city's walls bristling with defensive enhancements crafted by the Cyborg and his engineers.

The edge of the city, the open fields, had been transformed into battlegrounds. I, L.E.O., the Scarecrow, T.O.T.O., and my newly repaired Cyborg stood at the front. Our figures are stark against the morning light that struggled to pierce the gathering storm. Behind us, ranks of Citrusian volunteers, trained hastily but determined, readied themselves with weapons gleaming with bioluminescent energy.

The ground trembles beneath our feet as the Tangarmarine army approaches, their numbers far greater than any scout reports suggest. The air fills with the sour scent of aggression and rotting fruit. A stark contrast to the lemony freshness that pervades the city. At the head of the army, the Sorceress rides a chariot pulled by two giant Tangarmarine Beasts.

The Sorceress' skin is as pale as moonlight, contrasting starkly against the deep, midnight black of her long, flowing hair, which absorbs light rather than reflects it on the battlefield.

Her eyes are piercing and crimson. They glow with an inner fire of hatred.

Her attire is as dramatic as when she spoke to me for the first time: a cloak of shifting shadows that moves independently of any breeze, adorned with runes and symbols that glow with an eerie, blood-red light. Beneath this cloak, elegant armor, both elegant and menacing, crafted from a dark, metallic substance that seems to shift and change form.

Walking off the chariot, she gets down and looks right at me.

It begins.

***

The Tangarmarine army that stands on the horizon is composed of creatures both bizarre and terrifying in appearance and abilities. They are monstrous entities that are the backbone of their assault forces.

The Tangarmarine beast creature is large. The size of an Earth rhinoceros, with thick, tough rind skin that glows with a sickly orange hue. Their bodies are heavily armored with natural, chitinous plates that give them a jagged, menacing look. These plates are especially concentrated along their backs and flanks, protecting against attacks from above and behind. The beasts have eight legs, each ending in sharp, clawed feet, allowing them to maneuver over difficult terrain. Their heads are elongated, with glowing, neon orange eyes and a mouth full of razor-sharp teeth, capable of tearing through metal and flesh alike. A trio of tusk-like protrusions curve upwards from their jaws to go after their opponents in battle.

The Tangarmarine army of soldiers resembles a large, grotesque, moldy, humanoid orange. They stand on two legs and possess two arms, but their skin is a deep, blood-orange color, tough and leathery, with sporadic, spiky growths that serve as natural armor. Their faces are gruesome with no visible nose or ears, just slits where those features should be, and a wide mouth filled with small, sharp teeth. Their eyes are black, beady, and glossy, devoid of pupils, giving them a soulless gaze. Each soldier is equipped with weapons forged from the minerals of their planet, swords, spears, and shields that carry a corrosive aura, capable of eating through the armor and flesh of their enemies.

The aerial units add a critical dimension to the Tangarmarine army's capabilities. Resembling oversized, mutated bats with the texture and color of tangerines, these flyers have wingspans that can reach up to ten feet across. Their bodies secrete a sticky, acidic substance that helps them adhere to almost any surface, making them excellent at ambushing from above. Their heads are small and dominated by a large mouth that can spew corrosive spit over a distance, weakening enemy fortifications before ground troops move in.

Among the Tangarmarine ranks, there are specialized members known as Fleeters. These beings are smaller and less imposing than their brethren, with deep, translucent orange skin that seems to pulse with internal light. They do not engage directly in combat; rather, their role is strategic; they possess the ability to sense enemy movements and intentions, often guiding the Tangarmarine forces with uncanny accuracy. Fleeters are guarded zealously by other Tangarmarines, as their abilities are crucial for coordinating large-scale assaults and retreats.

The Tangarmarine army moves as a single, cohesive unit. Their actions have a hive-mind in execution. Driven by an insatiable desire to conquer and consume, controlled by the Sorceress who fills them with lies and deception.

***

At the forefront of the battlefield is L.E.O., whose upgrades are about to be assessed in the crucible of battle.

The evil forces approach in a menacing wave, their movements synchronized in a terrifying display of unity. As they close in, L.E.O. activates his enhanced projection core, casting multiple images of himself across the battlefield. These holograms move with lifelike precision, drawing the fire of the Tangarmarine archers and causing confusion within their ranks. Each decoy roars defiantly, a sound amplified to resonate across the fields, shaking the ground and morale of the enemy.

I raise my arm, signaling the Citrusians to hold their ground. Beside me, Cyborg's systems whir softly, calculating trajectories and wind speeds for optimal firing accuracy.

Tangarmarines surge forward, clashing violently against the city's defenses. Bio-engineered vines from the orb shot up from the ground, entangling the attackers, while Citrusian archers fired volleys of sharp seeds, falling scores of Tangarmarines with deadly precision.

Amid the chaos, T.O.T.O darts agilely between my legs and targets the Tangarmarines, disabling them with their bites and tactical interference. His metallic body, though small, was a blur of motion, weaving through the melee to drag injured Citrusians to safety and snapping fiercely at the heels of the advancing enemy.

In one pivotal moment, T.O.T.O. was sur-rounded by elite Tangarmarine warriors. Just as they close in, the Scarecrow, monitoring the field, quickly redirects its focus towards T.O.T.O's coordinates. He launches a precisely timed missile that explodes near the group, creating a smokescreen that allows T.O.T.O. to escape and regroup.

The Sorceress, not to be outdone, unleashes a powerful spell from her vantage point, dark energy bolts slicing through the air towards me and my friends. The Scarecrow, moving with surprising agility, intercepts many of these, its body absorbing the dark magic.

As the Citrusians rally on, L.E.O. uses his audio output to generate a series of disorienting roars and battle cries, creating a sonic barrier that momentarily disorients the attackers. The Citrusians use this opportunity to push back, driving the Tangarmarines away with a spirited counter-charge.

***

Hours have passed. The battlefield is riddled with the dead from both sides.

I wield my sword, crafted from a hardened citrus tree bark. Given as a gift from the mayor, it engages the evil forces, slicing them with great force.

The Cyborg is fighting relentlessly, powering high-intensity blasting rows of Tangarmarines upon contact with his laser eye.

I stand exposed to the battlefield and the Sorcerous, amid fallen bodies.

Cyborg jumps in front, just as the Sorceress fires a fatal blow. He protected the blast from her hand that was directed at me. The impact sends him crashing to the ground, its systems sparking erratically.

"NO!" I scream, running to Cyborg's side and deflecting incoming attacks. L.E.O., projecting himself between the fallen Cyborg and the Sorceress, tries to shield us with his own body, his form flickering violently under the onslaught of dark magic.

The Scarecrow lunges at the Sorceress, its body crackling with the absorbed energy, delivering a powerful blow that knocks her onto the ground. The battlefield falls silent as the Sorceress struggles to her feet, her cloak torn, and her face contorted in rage.

"You will not defeat me, Dotty, you fool!" she hisses, her hands glowing with dark energy. But before she can unleash her spell, I am upon her.

With a cry that blended fury and desperation, I swung my sword in a wide arc. The blade, glowing with a light as bright as the Citrusian suns, strikes the Sorceress squarely in the chest. A shockwave of energy explodes from the impact, sending ripples through the ground and knocking me and both armies off their feet.

The Sorceress looks down at the glowing wound with shock and realization. "This cannot be..." she stammers, her body beginning to dissolve into shadows that whisk her away in the wind, her scream begins fading into nothingness. Her army dissolves into the air just like particles of dust, as if this were a nightmare.

The battle is over. The city lay in partial ruins, and many had fallen, including the brave cyborg, who, though severely damaged, was still clinging to life. I kneel beside him, my eyes brimming with tears as the engineers rush to assess the damage.

"You saved me." I ran my hands through his hair, holding him close. Cyborg's eye flickers weakly. "I will save you now. Just hold on," I whisper to him.

Everyone near him who is left on the battle-field begins to lift him, including Scarecrow, and they take him away to engineering.

As I gaze out through the infirmary window, where they have transferred Cyborg to heal his human wounds, I look over the fields now marred by the vestiges of battle.

Beyond the horizon, the quartet of suns is positioned strategically across the sky like sentinels at the corners of the world; they finally pierce through the lingering veil of dark clouds.

The four suns bathe the ravaged landscape in a cascading warmth of healing light. This gentle illumination of golden and tender kisses of the broken planet transforms the fields into a canvas of stark contrasts. The shadows are retreating, and what was once a scene of desolation begins to heal.

I look up at the orb and see light, hugging everything around it. But the pain in my heart is for my beloved friend and lover.

Chapter 13

Bittersweet

In the aftermath of the fierce battle that has swept through the Citrusian city, the air is thick with the scent of burnt orange foliage, a reminder of the violence that has recently shaken the foundations of this peaceful society. The city bears scars of the conflict, with damaged buildings and scorched patches of earth vividly illustrating the battle's intensity.

Amidst the destruction, there's a palpable sense of relief and tentative hope. The Tangarmarine threat has been repelled and the Sorceress vanquished. The cost is evident in every weary face and tearful reunion in the city squares. Some have had to say goodbye to loved ones.

I wandered in the bustling medical center in one of the City's less damaged sectors, a temporary sanctuary for the wounded and a hub of ceaseless activity. The medical staff, augmented by sophisticated Citrusian healing technologies, move among the injured. Their hands and instruments are a blur of motion as they work to heal flesh, mend bone. In some cases, recalibrate mechanical limbs or circuitry.

In a quiet corner of this hive of healing, the Cyborg lies on a makeshift bed. He's wired to machines as a team of engineers collaborate with medical technicians to repair the damage he has sustained in the battle.

Cyborg's once immaculate metal surface is marred by scorch marks and dents, a testament to his bravery and the ferocity of the fight.

I approach quietly, tracing the familiar lines of his form, feeling a pang of distress at the sight of his wounds. As I reach his side, one of the engineers steps back, giving me space and a nod of acknowledgment. The room falls silent around me as I take his hand, his touch melts me.

"You fought bravely," I say softly, my voice thick with emotion. Cyborg's head turns slightly to regard me; his optic sensors dim but focused.

"I would do anything for you," he replies, his voice soft and muted. "To protect all of you, to protect... you, Dotty."

I squeeze his hand, my heart swelling with admiration and sorrow. "And you did. You saved us all. I..." I pause, my throat tight, my next words feeling monumental as they hover on the brink of utterance. "I love you," I confess, the words slipping out in a whisper, as if the admission could somehow make him more vulnerable.

His sensors flicker, a sign of his surprise but happiness in his smile. "Dotty, I love you too."

Cyborg gently squeezes my hand, an action filled with as much warmth and affection as he can muster.

"Dotty," he says, his voice steadier now. "Your presence has redefined my existence. You've given me a heart, in a way, and so much more than I never thought possible."

I look deeply into his eyes. The soft glow of his sensors reflects my own complex emotions. "And you've given me courage," I respond, my voice soft but filled with conviction. "Courage to face whatever comes. We're in this together, no matter where it leads." Gently, I lean over him and kiss his lips. He reaches for me to hold me closer.

I lay beside him in his medical bed in silence, each processing the hours of horror and emotions from the war. Around them, the medical center continues to buzz with activity, but within their small bubble, it's so peaceful. The engineer returns, breaking the moment with a respectful nod. "He's stable and should recover fully with some rest," he informs me, indicating Cyborg.

"You should both get some rest as well. Tomorrow the city will celebrate, and there will be much to do."

I stand up with a reluctant sigh, staring at Cyborg. "I'll be back first thing in the morning. Try to get some rest, okay?"

The Cyborg nods, his sensors dimming slightly as he settles back against the bedding. Programmed to conserve energy and expedite the healing process. "Stay with me tonight," he says softly.

"Of course. I will, but no funny business. I want you well enough so I can ravage you and make you scream." I wink.

Cyborg chuckles in response, "Yes, ma'am."

***

The Mayor of the city approaches me outside the next evening. His gait measured, his expression somber yet relieved, as he stops before me.

"Miss Dotty," he begins, his voice carrying the weight of his office and the recent strife. "You and your friends do a great service to Citria. Not just in defending us from the Tangarmarines but in showing us the strength of unity and courage. As promised, we are prepared to honor our commitment to you, to help you return home."

My eyes widen. A mix of relief and sudden apprehension flooded through me. The prospect of leaving, of saying goodbye to this world, seems suddenly bittersweet.

"Thank you, Mayor," I manage to say, my mind racing with the implications of his words. "I… I need some time to think about everything."

"Of course," the Mayor replies, understanding in his gaze. "Take all the time you need. We owe you that and much more."

As the Mayor walks away, leaving me with her tumultuous thoughts.

The city outside is slowly transitioning from the chaos of recovery to the quiet of night. Lights flicker in the homes and streets, casting a gentle glow that promises peace, at least for now. I take a deep breath of the cool night air, my mind replaying the Cyborg's words, he loves me. A smile touches my lips, a smile of someone who has found something unexpected and precious amid turmoil.

I walk back to my quarters, my steps light, and my heart full. Tonight, I hold onto the feeling of belonging, love, and the promise of a future filled with possibilities. I was told that tomorrow will come with demands, celebrations, and inevitable challenges. I received good news. Cyborg is on the mend, which makes me happy. I left him to mend and promised to return in the morning.

As I drift off to sleep, I am awoken by a soft tap on the door. T.O.T.O, resting on the carpet by my bed, barks once to let me know.

"Thank you, T.O.T.O., I wonder who that could be at this hour," I say to the dog as I open the door.

"Hi." Cyborg is standing there holding a bouquet of Cintria flowers.

"Hi!" I reach over to wrap my arms around his neck, kissing him gently, wearing nothing but a t-shirt. "Why aren't you resting? Did you escape? I have to take you back if you did. I want you well."

"I am more than okay. I got the all clear. I even asked if it was okay.. to, you know.. I will need to go slow, but I can. What are you wearing? Do you always answer the door like that?"

"Maybe.. why?" I laugh.

"Cause I am already feeling like I won't be able to go slow. Not with you looking this beautiful." He says, lifting my shirt to reveal that I am not wearing panties.

"Mm, have you come to give me sweet dreams tonight?" I grin.

"I am going to do much more than that. He says, grabbing my ass and pulling me close, closing the room door and lifting me, walking me to my bed.

I gently bite his ear and moan, wrapping my arms around him. "Yes, please."

On the bed, I slip off my shirt, revealing my excited, hard nipples. He took them in his mouth gently at first, cupping them with both hands, kissing me all over my body. He makes a kissing trail down my stomach, down the curve of my hip.

Every inch he is feeling with his hands and tongue. I moan loudly when his lips reach my center, kissing and licking. I shudder with every flick of his tongue. Climaxing, I grab the sheets, scream out, my whole body shaking.

"You taste delicious." He smiles, kissing me where he's pleased me.

"Now it's my turn to taste you," I say as I push him onto the bed.

"Mm, yes, please." Cyborg growls.

***

Chapter 14

The Mayor's Promise

The city, now quiet, the echoes of war slowly fading into the background, is a place of healing and rebuilding. The people of Citria work to repair their homes and lives..

The Mayor of Citria is both respected and burdened with the weight of his responsibilities, and summons me to the Capitol Building, a structure that miraculously survived the onslaught. The building, with its walls embedded with luminescent yellow stones. It is a beacon of Citrusian resilience.

My steps echo through the marble hall of the Mayor's mansion. I am led into a vast, dome-shaped room at the heart of the building, where the Mayor waits. He stands by a large oval window, gazing at the cityscape, his posture reflective. "Dotty," he begins, turning as I approach. His expression is earnest, tinged with a somberness appropriate for the trials they have all endured. "Your bravery and wisdom have given us a second chance. A chance to restore what was lost.

For that, we are eternally grateful, I am eternally grateful."

I nod, "Thank you, Mayor. I did what I felt was right, what I had to do," my thoughts drifting momentarily to my ache for home that is not forgotten.

The Mayor walks toward me, his hands clasped behind his back. "And now, it is time for us to fulfill our promise, to help you return to your home. This has been my commitment to you from the start."

I feel a flutter of hope. But it is mixed with an inexplicable sense of foreboding. I watch him closely, trying to read the layers beneath his formal demeanor.

"As you know," the Mayor continues, "our technologies and magics are powerful and varied. We have delved into every tome, consulted every sage, and researched every artifact that might aid us in deciphering the path back to your world." He pauses, his gaze meeting mine with an intensity that makes my heart beat even faster. "However, the truth we have uncovered is more complex than anticipated."

My heart sinks, a chill passing through me despite the warm room. "What do you mean?" I ask, my voice barely above a whisper.

The Mayor sighs, turning to look out the window again. "Our world, Citria, is connected to others through a network of light, the very light that leads you here to this planet. But these pathways are not easily navigated or reversed. The beacon you saw was not a doorway but a mirror, reflecting not the route to other worlds but the energy within our own."

He faces me again, his expression lined with regret. "In simpler terms, Dotty, while we can send you into the orb, we cannot guarantee that it will lead you home. It has never been used in such a way, and to attempt it without certainty..." He trails off, leaving the unspoken risks hanging between them.

I process his words; my mind is racing. The revelation that my journey home might remain out of reach is a bitter pill. I feel the walls of the room closing in around me, a sense of isolation creeping into my heart.

"That would explain why I've never seen your planet on our maps. But there must be some other way?" I press him, my desperation clear.

The Mayor nods slowly, "We have one possibility, it's an ancient artifact.. But its location, let alone its existence, has never been confirmed. It is a tale passed down through generations, often dismissed as folklore.

The artifact is not merely a relic but a key, literally and figuratively, to accessing deeper layers of control and communication with the orb. According to ancient Citria lore, the articfact is part of the original structure which contained the Citrus Core, serving as a conduit for its energy and a controller for its immense power."

My mind latches onto this sliver of hope. "Then I'll find it. It's worth the risk if there's even a chance…" My voice is determined; my resolve hardens.

The Mayor studies me for a moment, then nods in agreement. "Very well. I will provide you with all the resources you need for this quest. Maps, guides, supplies, there is everything at our disposal. If there is a way to find this Core, we will find it together."

***

As Dotty and her friends leave the Capitol, the weight of her continued journey on Citria settles on her shoulders. The city around her, bathed in the fading light of dusk, seems both beautiful and daunting. Yet, as she walks through the streets, the citizens nodding to her with respect and whispered blessings, Dotty feels a surge of determination. Citria is no longer just the world she landed in by chance; it has become a part of her story, who she is.

And somewhere out there, amid a vast wilderness and hidden secrets of this alien home, a path must be forged to find home.

Chapter 15

Find me where the lemons grow

Dotty and her friends prepare for their expedition a few weeks later. Their mission is to locate the legendary artifact of Citria, rumored to have the power to bridge worlds.

Before leaving, they gather at the city's edge, where the Mayor and a crowd of citizens come to see them off. The Mayor hands Dotty a sealed scroll containing information and maps that detail their best guesses about the Core's possible location.

The Mayor's voice resonates with solemnity. "May the light guide you, and may the shadows flee from your path."

Dotty nods her brow, sweating in the heat of the sun, and tucks the scroll into her pack. "We'll find the Core and return; you have my word."

As the group sets out, the terrain of Citria begins to change, from the lush, vibrant forests surrounding the city to the more rugged, untamed wilderness that lies beyond. The air grows cooler, and the scent of the unknown wafts on the breeze.

L.E.O. takes the lead, his form flickering slightly in the morning light. His upgraded systems allow him to scan the environment and overlay maps directly onto the terrain, providing real-time navigation advice.

As they approach a particularly dense thicket, L.E.O. halts, his sensors picking up movement. "Remember, if you ever get lost in the woods, freeze your compass, get hypothermia, and you'll stop being lost," he quips, causing Dotty to roll her eyes.

"Is now really the time for dad jokes, L.E.O.?" she chuckles, despite the tension of their mission.

"It's always the time," L.E.O. responds with a simulated smirk. "Laughter is the best way to keep the fear at bay."

The Scarecrow, ever the strategist, keeps close to Dotty, his sensors continuously analyzing the terrain for threats. His missile launchers are ready, not for attack. But, as a deterrent, they should encounter hostile wildlife or residual Tangarmarine forces.

At one point, when a shadowy figure darts in the distance, the Scarecrow's quick analysis confirms it's just a native animal. "All clear." He reassured the group, "Just a Citria shadow cat, more afraid of us than we are of it."

T.O.T.O., with his enhanced sensors and agility, scouts ahead, darting back and forth between the trees. As they reach a clearing marked on one of their maps as a point of interest, T.O.T.O. circles, sniffing the ground and occasionally digging lightly before looking up at Dotty with excitement.

"This might be it," Dotty says, kneeling to examine the ground where T.O.T.O. has stopped. "The soil here is different, loose, as if it's been disturbed."

Cyborg analyzes the ground. "It's been turned over recently. Let's set up a temporary camp here and explore more thoroughly tomorrow since it's getting dark."

"Good idea, I could use a little nap," winking at Cyborg.

Scarecrow and L.E.O. look at each other and laugh.

"What?" Dotty and Cyborg say at the same time.

***

As the sun sets, painting the sky in shades of orange and purple, the rest of the group shares a quiet meal, a feast provided by the Mayor's ambassador. Only the finest foods, Citria rainbow barley stew, and citrus candied fruit for dessert.

That night, as they sit around a small fire, L.E.O. projects images of ancient Citria lore into the air, the stories woven with hints of the Core's significance. "Legends say it was not just a source of power, but a beacon of peace, bringing balance where there was discord," L.E.O. narrates, his voice distant.

"We should have looked for that relic before knowing that. Well, no matter what happens, we're at least we are together," she states, a warm smile on her face. Looking around at her companions, snuggled up to Cyborg. His arms wrapped around her, giving her a gentle squeeze at the remark. She thinks to herself that each of them is so different.

The next morning, the journey leads them to a secluded valley rumored in ancient texts as "the place where the lemons grow," a site of old Citria lore and guarded secrets.

The valley's air feels thick, the scent of the citrus vegetation. A sharp yet sweet fragrance that heightens senses and fills them with a sense of eerie anticipation. Tall tree trunks, thick and twisted, stretch toward the sky, their branches heavy with bright, alien lemons that glow softly in the morning light.

"Looks like we're in the right place," Dotty murmurs, her gaze sweeping over the grove with awe and curiosity. The scene is stark, almost surreal, with the golden fruits casting a luminous pall over the soft, verdant undergrowth.

As they press forward, the soft hum of Citria wildlife around them, T.O.T.O leads, his sensors twitching and adjusting with every step. The Scarecrow keeps a watchful eye on their surroundings.

L.E.O., projecting historical data and lore about the valley, speaks in a low, reverent tone, "This grove was once considered sacred by the ancients of Citria. They believed it to be a place of power and hidden wisdom."

Dotty, equipped with a handheld scanner, starts examining the base of the largest lemon trees, where the ground is soft and undisturbed. The scanner beeps rhythmically, the pitch rising as she nears the center of the groove.

Suddenly, the device lets out a long, high-pitched tone, indicating something significant beneath the soil. With careful hands, Dotty begins to dig, her fingers brushing against something hard and cold. As she clears the dirt, a metallic object, intricately carved and pulsating with a soft, lemon-hued light, emerges from the earth.

"It's here... the artifact!" Dotty exclaims, her voice a mix of triumph and disbelief.

The group gathers around, staring at the object in wonder. The artifact, shaped like a lemon but much larger, is covered in ancient Citria runes that glow softly upon touch.

***

Cyborg steps closer to me, now alone since L.E.O. and Scarecrow went to wash the artifact at a nearby creek. His movements are deliberate. "Dotty," he begins, his voice steady but filled with emotion. Throughout our journey, I understand more than just strategies and battle tactics. From you, I have learned what it means to care, to feel connection... to love, even without the new software, I believe, no matter what, that I love you more and more every day, Dotty. I couldn't imagine my life without you."

I turn to face him. The Citria light filtering through the leaves, casting dappled patterns on his metallic and skin meshed frame, softening the lines of his once purely utilitarian form. "I feel the same, my love," I say softly, my heart beating faster.

I reached out, my hand touching his arm, feeling his strength. "I'm glad you're here, with me, I knew, and I felt it when I met you. I love you." I kiss him slowly. Passionately tasting him, mouths open, exploring with tongues.

T.O.T.O. nudges Cyborg's leg and breaks up the intense moment. He bends to scratch under the dog's chin.

Scarecrow adjusts his stance, looking between Dotty and the Cyborg with a thoughtful expression. Hearing the conversation in the distance when he returns to the campsite, Scarecrow says, "Well, my friend," addressing the Cyborg with a warm tone, "it seems that amidst all our battles and searches, there's more than just relics and artifacts to be found. There's also heart, even where we least expect it. And I should know since my programming is complete."

Cyborg nods slowly. "It seems so. A great brain you have is what my human cyborg friends of long ago used to say, Scarecrow!"

L.E.O. projects a smile. "Isn't this the most unexpected journey of all? But let's not forget, we still have quite a trek back to the city. And I, for one, can't wait to see what tales they'll tell of our adventures in the future!" He beams broadly, his holographic form flickering slightly with enthusiasm.

I chuckle, the tension easing from my shoulders. "I'm sure your version will have a bit more... flair, L.E.O."

"Oh, absolutely, Dotty!" L.E.O. agrees, his voice ringing with mirth. "Imagine the epic sagas we'll inspire. 'Me, the brave adventurer, and our quest for the Citrus of destiny.' It has a nice ring to it, doesn't it?"

Scarecrow, who has been quietly listening and analyzing, adds perspective. "It's not just about the tales we tell or the artifacts we find. It's about how we change along the way. Look at us! A human, a hologram, a scarecrow, and a robotic dog. United by a common goal. It's poetic."

T.O.T.O barks in agreement, wagging his tail energetically as if to punctuate Scarecrow's words.

I nod, my gaze sweeping over these wonderful companions. "We started this as a mission to get me home, but it's become much bigger. You've all shown me parts of Citria, and yourselves, that I couldn't have imagined when I first crashed here."

As we walk back, the conversation shifts to planning our next steps. We discuss how we should present the artifact to the city's scholars and engineers. I am hoping its secrets can be unlocked safely and lead to more clues about the mysterious Core of Citria.

"The road ahead might be daunting, "I say as we navigate through the lush underbrush, "but I think we're ready for whatever comes next. After all, we're not just a team; we've become a family."

The path winds before us, shaded by the towering trees and lit by the occasional ray of sunlight piercing through the canopy.

As we approach the City, the familiar sights and sounds of Citria welcome us back to the gate. The guard is much friendlier than before, letting us in without hesitation.

***

Chapter 16

When life gives you lemons

Dotty and her friends return to the Citrusian city, carrying the mysterious artifact from the valley of the lemons, which creates a stir among the inhabitants and the governing council.

The news of their discovery spreads quickly, igniting a mixture of excitement and apprehension throughout the populace.

The Mayor, ever the composed leader, organizes a team of the city's best engineers and scholars to examine the artifact and explore its capabilities, all in hopes of fulfilling the promise made to Dotty, to find a way to send her home.

In the city's Capitol, the grand hall, the artifact is carefully placed on a specially designed platform surrounded by equipment and monitors. The team, led by the Mayor himself, works tirelessly to blend science and ancient Citrusian lore.

The Mayor, understanding the significance of this moment, oversees the operations, ensuring every measure is taken to unlock the secrets of the artifact safely.

As the engineers work, they discover that the artifact is not merely a relic but a complex device capable of manipulating dimensional energies, creating stable portals for other worlds. This revelation brings a new level of urgency to their efforts. The Mayor, aware of the implications, discusses the next steps with his team.

"We must proceed with caution," he advises, his voice steady despite the excitement buzzing around the room. "This device could be the key to not only sending Dotty home but also understanding the fabric of our universe through the orb."

Cyborg finds himself worried. He approaches her as she watches the engineers work, his voice soft yet firm.

"Dotty, if this device can take you home, I will follow as I promised. And if not, we will build a new home here, on Citria."

Dotty turns to face him, moved by his declaration. "I am so glad, cause I want to be with you. I want to raise our baby together," she responds, touching her belly.

"Are you? Oh, Dotty, I love you so much," Cyborg says, embracing her. His voice tinged with emotion, "I belong with you, here or anywhere, for our family." He wraps his arms around her and kisses her softly.

Upon hearing their exchange, L.E.O. struggles with his conflicting emotions. As a guardian of Citria, he has to protect the city and its people, including Dotty. Yet, losing her to another world fills him with sadness.

"Dotty, while I wish for your happiness with Cyborg, know that your presence has brightened Citria in ways that we could not have imagined," L.E.O. expresses, his holographic form flickering with uncharacteristic somberness. "Your leaving would dim the light you've brought here. Plus, I want to spoil him or her when it comes time. But now, it is selfish to keep you here."

Scarecrow joins the conversation with a pragmatic approach. "Perhaps there's a way to replicate the artifact's technology," he suggests. "If we could understand its mechanics fully, maybe we could create a method for you to visit, rather than permanently leave."

Dotty listens to her friends, each offering their perspective and support. Her heart swells with gratitude for these bonds formed in such unusual circumstances. "Thank you, all of you," she says, her voice thick with emotion. "Let's focus on understanding this artifact first. Then, we'll decide the best course together."

The engineers initiate a controlled activation of the artifact, which emits a soft, pulsing glow, its energy patterns displaying a complex network of potential gateways.

Witnessing the test, the Mayor realizes the gravity of their discovery. "We are on the brink of something monumental," he announces. "This artifact doesn't just open pathways; it will connect lives and destinies."

As the test concludes, the room bursts into cautious optimism.

The Mayor, looking more solemn than usual, steps forward. His hands are clasped tightly behind his back, his gaze fixed on the glowing artifact. He clears his throat, commanding the attention of everyone in the room. "I have something to confess before we proceed," the Mayor begins, his voice steady but filled with an uncharacteristic heaviness. The room falls silent, the hum of machinery the only sound accompanying his words.

"This artifact was not new as you were led to believe. It was found many years ago, during the early days of my administration. I had it hidden. I did not know how to use its power and feared it.

I now believe that the artifact represents knowledge, power, and responsibility. Its connection with the orb, a source of life and balance for Citria, emphasizes themes of guardianship, wisdom, and the ethical use of power. Dotty, the artifact's reunion and activation will function, I hope, as a bridge between our worlds."

Surprised murmurs ripple through the room. Dotty exchanges a puzzled look with her companions, her mind racing to piece together the implications of his words.

The Mayor continues, "I was young and overwhelmed by responsibility and leadership. When this artifact was unearthed, I was terrified of its potential, terrified it would bring disaster rather than benefit. I hid it, claiming it was lost, hoping one day, someone wiser and more capable could unlock its secrets."

He pauses, looking around at the faces of his team, faces filled with shock, but also understanding. "I am deeply ashamed of my actions. But seeing you here, Dotty, with the courage and intelligence that I lacked, I am hopeful. Hopeful that you can correct the mistakes of my past."

Dotty steps forward, her initial shock giving way to empathy. "We all have fears, Mayor," she says gently. "But it wasn't right to make this whole journey up. We went and looked for it, believing in you."

"I know, even when you set off, I wanted to stop you, to tell you the truth, but my feet were planted firmly on the ground. I had been telling the lie for far too long."

Nodding gratefully at Dotty, the Mayor looks at the engineers. "Let us proceed. Let's find out what this artifact's power truly holds."

The engineers activate the controls, and the artifact begins to pulse more intensely, its light filling the room with a warm, golden hue. The sensors relay data rapidly to the monitors, showing fluctuating energy patterns and potential dimensional coordinates.

Suddenly, the artifact stabilizes, projecting a clear, stable gateway in the middle of the room. A swirling vortex of light that promises passage to unknown realms, connecting it all from the glowing orb.

The Mayor steps closer, his earlier apprehension replaced by a resolve born of redemption. "I will go through first," he declares. "If there is any danger, it should be mine to face, Dotty."

Before anyone can protest, he steps into the vortex. For a moment, he is enveloped in the brilliant light, and then he vanishes, leaving a stunned silence in his wake.

The hours ticked by. Each minute stretching into eternity as the team waited with bated breath. Then, just as suddenly as he had disappeared, the Mayor re-emerges from the vortex, unharmed and with a look of awe, his hair now a brilliant glow.

"It's amazing, I have seen so much," he announces, his voice filled with wonder. "The portal led to a breathtaking planet, unlike any I've ever seen. The artifact works, it truly works. Oh, the places I have been!"

The room erupts in cheers and applause, relief and excitement mingling. Dotty smiles, her heart swelling with pride and hope, not just for herself but all of Citria.

The Mayor approaches Dotty, his expression sincere. "Dotty, with this success, we can send you home. We will try and channel it directly to your planet. We owe you a debt of gratitude for bringing us to this point. Do you wish to go now?"

Dotty nods, her thoughts turning to her friends, Cyborg, L.E.O., and Scarecrow. "Thank you, Mayor," she glances at her companions, "this feels a lot like home already, but I am sure my family is worried."

The Mayor nods understandingly, sighing with relief and a tinge of sadness. "Of course, Dotty."

Chapter 17

Farewell to thee

Scarecrow, ever the thinker, speaks with a practical tone. "We'll need to ensure the portal's stability for a return, should you wish to visit. I'll collaborate with the engineers to establish a safe and reliable way to keep the pathways open. It's important to all of us that you have options to return."

I nod appreciatively, touched by Scarecrow's foresight.

"Thank you, Scarecrow. That means everything to me. Knowing I can come back makes this a lot easier."

A week later, the community of Citria gathers to bid farewell to me. Emotions run high as I hug so many friends I have made, each embrace lingering a little longer than usual.

Cyborg at my side, ready to step through the portal with me. I take one last look at the faces in the crowd. The faces that have become dear to me, I consider family.

"See you later," I whisper, a promise hanging in the air.

Cyborg and I stand hand-in-hand, the portal stabilizes into a shimmering gateway, ready to step through. The air is filled with anticipation, and the Citrusians watch with bated breath. Just as we are about to enter the swirling light, a sudden alarm blares from one of the monitoring stations.

One of the engineers rushes forward, a look of urgent concern on her face. "Wait!" she calls out, causing us to halt abruptly. The crowd falls silent, turning their attention to the engineer now examining her data pad frantically.

"There's a problem," they announce. "The portal's energy matrix isn't compatible with non-organic materials. It's fluctuating dangerously whenever it interacts with Cyborg's metal components."

The revelation hits like a physical blow, and a hush falls over the crowd. My heart sinks, my eyes meet Cyborg's, which display an unmistakable flash of disappointment.

"I'm sorry, Dotty," Cyborg says to me, his voice steady despite the clear turmoil. "I can't go with you. The risk of destabilizing the portal and endangering you and the baby is too great."

My dream of having Cyborg by my side and my return home is suddenly dashed, and I feel something more than disappointment. "Isn't there another way? Can't we modify the portal or something?" I plead, looking around at the assembled engineers and scientists.

Scarecrow steps forward, his expression grave. "We've tried to adjust the portal's parameters several times, but the fundamental nature of the energy it uses makes it unsafe to transport organic, synthetic, and metallic materials together. We need more time to research and invent new types of technology to overcome this flaw. Perhaps if you stay with us a little longer, Dotty, we can find a way."

L.E.O., ever the empathetic companion, floats closer, his form flickering slightly. "Dotty, we'll keep working on it. You should go home and see your family if it is safe. You will find us again just like before, just as the mayor returned to us. This isn't the end. If there's a way to bring him through safely, we will find it."

I nod, trying to muster a brave smile, knowing the reality of the situation. "I know you will. And I'll be waiting," I say, knowing this was a once-in-a-lifetime miracle that I came to this planet. Is it safe for me to enter or return in my condition?"

"I don't think it would be wise until you have had the child to return, if you decide to go. We don't know what it will do to the fetus when you are inside the portal, our research is too new. You are taking a chance; it is a risk, either way. This is your decision."

I turn to Cyborg. "I don't know if I can have the baby without you being a part of it. I should stay here with you, especially if it might not be safe."

Cyborg nods solemnly. "I will be here, working on a solution from this side. I'll never stop trying, for as long as it takes. But you should go to your family now and let them know you are okay. They must be worried, I am sure it must be safe, the Mayor seems fine."

My heart is shattering into a thousand pieces. This was not the answer I wanted or expected him to say. My decision is made. He wants me to go. I will go. I hug Cyborg, but I cannot kiss him, no, not like this. I embrace him, feeling his arms and warmth, a stark reminder of the barrier between us.

"It's time to make a choice, it seems as though we cannot maintain a strong signal to your world much longer, like we thought," the Mayor says softly, gesturing towards the portal, "I am sorry, Dotty. We may not get our chance again for a long time. You need to decide. We cannot guarantee safety to pass through."

With one last look back at my friends, I decide I have no choice now, not if I may never be able to see my family, I need to go home. I step into the portal alone. I can't risk staying, not for him, never to return home. The light envelops me, and with a final wave, I disappear, and everything turns a brilliant white.

The portal stops working abruptly, smoke filling the skyline. The crowd watching gaps and goes silent, not knowing whether Dotty has made it. Cyborg stands at the forefront, staring where Dotty disappeared, mind racing through possible technical solutions.

L.E.O. and Scarecrow join him, each placing a hand on his shoulder in a gesture of support. "We'll find a way to get it working again," L.E.O. reassures him.

"Yes," Scarecrow adds, "and Cyborg, we will be here for you. She may be there, but she's still part of this. A part of us, don't forget what the mayor said. She loves you. I am sure she made it through."

Cyborg, never taking his eyes off the portal, says with deep sadness and instant regret, "I do love her; she is my life. I should have told her to stay here. What have I done? Now.. everything is uncertain."

As the crowd disperses, the team heads back to their laboratories and workshops, and their mission is clear.

Back in Citria, as the light from the portal fades out, L.E.O., Scarecrow, and the others stand together, still watching where Dotty disappeared, hoping she would step back through the broken portal again one day.

Chapter 18

Squeeze lemon on those cuts

Six months have passed since Dotty stepped through the portal, leaving behind the world of Citria and her friends who had become as close as family.

Cyborg, ever diligent, spends countless hours in the laboratory alongside Citria's finest engineers and scientists, trying to find a way to modify his structure or the portal's. Each attempt, though innovative, fell short of allowing his safe passage through the portal. They cannot find the U.S.S. Kansas, it has disappeared.

One cool Citria evening, after another round of unsuccessful tests, Cyborg stood in the vast, now-quiet laboratory, staring at the dormant portal. The array of inactive screens and silent equipment mocked his efforts. A profound sense of solitude settled over him, magnifying the emptiness in the room.

The portal, a structure of complex machinery and pulsating energy conduits, had remained inactive since Dotty's departure. Cyborg's optical sensors lingered on the silent gateway, a portal representing both a barrier and a bridge to his heart's desire.

Driven by a mix of longing and frustration, Cyborg decided that if there was even the slightest chance he could withstand the portal's tumultuous energies, he had to take it. He started up the portal's control panel, the familiar hum of machinery filling the air, dispelling the silence. The patterns of the portal flickered to life, casting a swirling dance of lights across the lab walls.

L.E.O., who had been maintaining his nightly vigil at the lab, noticed the activation. His holographic form flickered into the room; surprise was evident in his voice. "Cyborg, what are you doing?"

"I have to try," Cyborg responded, his voice resolute. "I can't wait any longer, L.E.O. I need to see her, to be with her. What if there is something wrong with the baby? The theoretical models might not be ready, but I've adjusted to the system. It's now or never."

L.E.O., understanding the depth of his resolve, nodded slowly. "Very well, I'll monitor the energy fluctuations. If it becomes too unstable, I'll pull you back."

Cyborg approached the portal, the light from the gateway reflecting off his metallic frame. He paused at the threshold, taking a moment to look back at L.E.O. "Thank you, my friend. For understanding."

With a deep, steadying intake of his ventilation system, Cyborg stepped forward into the swirling vortex of the portal. The energy around him crackled and roared, enveloping his form in a brilliant glow. L.E.O. watched anxiously, monitoring the energy readings that spiked dangerously.

Cyborg felt a searing pain inside the portal as the incompatible energies interacted with his metallic parts. His vision blurred. The circuits started overheating, and the alarms rang in his auditory processors. Yet, amidst the chaos, his thoughts remained clear, focused on Dotty and the hope of reaching her.

At the lab, L.E.O. saw the critical warnings flash across the screens. "Hold on, Cyborg! I'm bringing you back!" L.E.O. activated the emergency retrieval system before the situation could escalate to a critical failure. The portal's energy reversed, and Cyborg was forcibly pulled back into the lab. Thrown back, he collapsed onto the floor, systems short-circuiting, his body smoking slightly from the ordeal.

L.E.O. rushed to his side, stabilizing his systems to prevent any more permanent damage. As Cyborg's sensors came online, he looked up at L.E.O., defeat in his stance.

"I had to try," he murmured, his voice weak. "For her."

T.O.T.O. licks Cyborg's face and lies beside him. "You miss her too, I know." T.O.T.O. whines and puts his head on Cyborg's belly.

L.E.O., his tone gentle, charged with worry, responded, "I know we all miss her, and we'll keep trying, my friend. Together, we'll find a way, you can't die on me now!"

Chapter 19

Vivid Dreaming

Dotty's return to the U.S.S. Kansas, her starship home stationed in orbit around a bustling trade route, was as unexpected as her departure. She materialized in the engineering bay and passed out. Everyone was rushing to her, not knowing where she had appeared from. He was in the medical ward for weeks before being released. Dotty explained that she went through a portal to get there, but no one believed her. Checking her brain for possible lesions. A negative result was shown, and she was released from the medical facility.

The familiar hum of the ship's reactors and the metallic scent of ionized air instantly grounded her as she walked home. The stark contrast between the vibrant, alien landscapes of Citria and the utilitarian, steel corridor on the ship was disorienting.

As she steadied herself, taking in her surroundings, leaving the medical ward, the door to the engineering bay slid open with a hiss. Her Aunt Marie and Uncle George, who also served on the ship as senior engineers, rushed in, their faces etched with concern and relief.

"Dotty!" Aunt exclaimed, rushing to embrace her. The reunion was emotional, filled with tears and laughter, holding Dotty tight. Their hands patted her back and checked her to confirm she was real and unharmed.

Uncle, always the more composed of the two, pulled back and looked at her with a scrutinizing gaze. "We thought you had an accident, kiddo. There was no storm the night you disappeared; an explosion was confirmed from the old shuttle you were in. Yet, they found you unconscious on the deck. We feared the worst."

Her Aunt nodded vigorously, still clutching Dotty's hand. "The medics said it might have been a fuel leak or something that knocked you out. You've been in a coma until now."

Dotty, processing their words, knew the truth stretched far beyond a simple accident. Her journey through dimensions, the friends she made, and the battles she fought were experiences that had changed her profoundly. She smiled softly, a mix of nostalgia and melancholy from the memories. "I've been on quite an adventure," she began, her voice low. "It's a long story, about places and friends far beyond what we know here."

Her relatives exchanged a look, a mixture of skepticism and intrigue on their faces. "Maybe you hit your head harder than we thought," The Uncle joked half-heartedly, though he tried not to, and showed genuine concern.

"No, really," Dotty insisted, her tone earnest. "I promise, it's all true. I'll explain everything, but it might take a while. I am pregnant."

Her Aunt Marie looked at her husband, George, and at Dotty. "I am so sorry, the doctors didn't tell you. You were bleeding when they found you. You had a miscarriage. I am surprised they didn't call us when you were released from the medical ward. I guess they didn't want to overwhelm you more than you needed." Dotty's Aunt took her hand and held it for a moment.

The shock of hearing the loss, the room spun, and she felt as if she was going to faint. "No, no, no, no! It was the only thing I had left of him." Crying into her hands, she said. The hurt and depression set in. "He didn't want me to stay anyway, I guess it's for the best."

Grabbing Dotty and hugging her tight, Marie spoke, "Don't you ever say such things. You mourn the loss of a life you didn't have the chance to raise. Don't try to logic your way out of feeling the pain of it and heal."

***

Over the next few months, Dotty tried to re-integrate into life aboard the U.S.S. Kansas, but her heart often wandered back to Citria. She missed Cyborg, L.E.O., T.O.T.O., and Scarecrow dearly, her comrades who had become like family. She thought of what it would have been like to have her child with her. Never having the chance to hold it or teach it things. It hurt more than any physical pain you could imagine.

She decided to have a small funeral for her unborn child. The empty casket was closure. Saying goodbye to a soul she had never met. But she imagined walking her to school and teaching her the alphabet. She even named her Chance. It was cathartic to give her a presence, an importance in her life.

***

Dotty began documenting her experiences a year after the funeral, compiling notes and sketches in a digital log. She detailed the technology of Citria, the creatures, the landscapes, and the critical moments of her journey. This log became her only connection to that other life, a reminder that her experiences were real and transformative.

Sometimes, during the quiet shifts in the engine room, Aunt Marie and Uncle George would find Dotty staring out into the star-filled void, her eyes filled with tears, her expression saddened. Dotty went back to the medical team and requested her test results. The tests revealed she was pregnant at one point. She had lost the baby. The doctors assumed she lost it from the ship crashing, and still couldn't account for the rest of how she got there. No ship. When she recanted her story, they looked at her strangely. They didn't press her for more stories, sensing that whatever Dotty had experienced was profound and deeply personal.

Sitting in the common room in the afternoon, watching the stars streak by from the viewing port, Dotty shared more about her adventures with her family. The lessons she learned, her plans to return to Citria one day, and Cyborg.

"Citria is part of me now. He is a part of me," Dotty admitted, her voice tinged with a resolve that surprised even her. "I left something important behind, and I intend to get it back, not just for me but for my friends and my love who is still there. I need clarity."

Aunty squeezed her hand, a supportive smile on her face. "Well, give it some time, dear. You never know what can happen. Time heals all."

Uncle George nodded, "That is true, we all have dreams and heartache. Give it some time. Everything softens with time. It will pass on to acceptance. Perhaps you can meet someone nice here."

Dotty shook her head; she didn't want to forget or put it in the past.

***

Many months later, one evening, I was conducting routine maintenance on the ship's communication array, and a series of unusual electrical fluctuations caught my attention. I resolved to get used to my day-to-day routine again, putting the memory of what happened on the back burner.

I continued to send encrypted messages into space, via deep-space communications. I am desperately trying to see if I could contact the planet of Citria. No response. It was like they never existed.

The console suddenly flickered erratically, initially emitting random noises. Upon closer inspection, I realized there was a pattern within the disturbance. A coded message was concealed in the static. As I deciphered it, my hands trembled slightly. I needed a moment to catch my breath.

The return message read: *"Not a dream. We await your return. We had trouble locating you once the portal closed. We just got the last signal to locate you. Cyborg is not well. –L.E.O."*

Goosebumps cover my skin as the reality of my adventures on Citria crashes back into my consciousness, sweeping away any lingering doubts.

The message is a lifeline, a confirmation that my time on that distant planet was real. I knew it was as real as the stars shining outside my window.

"I am coming, my love, hold on." Hugging myself.

Epilogue

In the dim light of her workshop aboard the U.S.S. Kansas, Dotty stood before a complex array of equipment that hummed with potential.

Around her, holographic displays floated, showing intricate diagrams that melded the cutting-edge of femtometer robotics with advanced biological science. The room was alive with a symphony of beeps and whirrs, each sounding a note in the grand composition that was her ambition.

Upon returning to Citria, the portal closed again, making it challenging to keep a signal from each planet. Dotty blacked out again, stepping through the portal. Why didn't this happen to the Mayor? She had to figure out how to have humans pass in and out without medical intervention, every time.

Dotty wanted it to be a smooth transition, not just through brute force technology, but through an elegant fusion of biology and mechanics.

The project was bold, revolutionary even. Dotty devised a plan to create a biotechnological conduit, a living, breathing portal anchored in both worlds by a genetically engineered citrus tree whose roots and branches extended through the fabric of space-time itself. This 'Quantum Arbor,' as she called it, was designed to be a permanent, stable link between planets, and a flourishing biosphere was specially constructed as a biosphere on the U.S.S. Kansas.

She adjusted the parameters on a particularly sensitive piece of equipment, the Quantum Arbor, at its nascent stage, pulsing softly in its containment unit. Its leaves and fruit shimmered with a metallic sheen; each imbued with millions of femto-circuits and mirrored the starry night sky. The whole idea had come to her in a dream, where the lines between organic and inorganic blurred, suggesting a harmony that could bridge worlds without the risk of destructive energy dissonance that regular portals presented.

The breakthrough had come from a dream about Citria itself and the orb. It was as if the orb had somehow channeled its way to her through a dream state as she slept.

The messages from her friends, encoded in botanical sequences, hinted at ancient Citria techniques of weaving life with technology, methods lost to time but reborn through her efforts.

With each new passing day, the Quantum Arbor of artificial intelligence grew stronger, its presence a testament to the union of Dotty's worlds.

But the project was not without its dangers. By integrating such potent technologies, any miscalculation could lead to a catastrophic unravelling of the very fabric of reality. Dotty was determined to make it work. Driven by memories of her friends and the promise she had made to them to return.

As the final preparations were made, Dotty reflected on the journey that had brought her here. The U.S.S. Kansas had become more than just a ship or her home; it was a cradle for a vision that could change the understanding of connection and distance.

Her aunt and uncle watched her work with a mixture of pride and much worry that she might be setting herself up for failure. But they saw her leave and return, so they believed her.

***

The stars watched me silently from high above, The Quantum Arbor is ready.

I initiate the activation sequence; my heart is pounding violently. The citrus tree began to glow, a soft, pulsing light grew steadily brighter.

Then, with a gentle sigh, the air smelled with the scent of an alien forest, the fruits glowed bright, and the portal opens.

Before me, a pathway to Citria unfolds. Through the portal, the air shimmers. I can see the lush landscapes and glowing butterfly-like creatures flying around my second home. The connection was stable. A beautiful blend of flora and tech married together, perfectly.

Stepping through, I find myself again on Citria soil. This time, I am not a crash-landed visitor; I don't black out. I am the bridge.

My aunt and uncle are thrilled and relieved for me, watching on the other side, I wave them to enter. Finally, it's safe.

As for my friends, T.O.T.O, Cyborg, L.E.O., and Scarecrow, all come into view, their expressions wide with astonishment.

I run to Cyborg, then halt. I pause and then utter the words I have wanted to say for over a year, "Why didn't you ask me to stay?"

"I didn't want you to regret your decision to stay here, away from your family. I only hoped you would stay."

"I wanted you to tell me you wanted me to stay." Dotty's eyes spilling tears," I lost our baby."

He grabs me in his arms and holds me tight. "I will never forgive myself. I am so sorry. Never again will you ever doubt me, I will live the rest of this life making it up to you and our lost one."

"Never again, together forever." I bury my head in his chest and cry, letting out and letting go of the pain. "Such a stupid thing we should have said to each other, lost in words in the moment for a lifetime of pain."

"I know. Even with machine enhancements, the human flaws of emotion can ruin a wonderful thing."

"It's not ruined. I still love you," I respond, teary-eyed, looking into Cyborg's eyes.

"I love you, too," he replied, kissing me deeply. He knew it was true with every circuit and DNA cell mixture within him.

Years later, I became a legend of cosmic proportions with this invention.

The portal has opened up to the vastness of the universe, and with this new tech, we can meet many other undiscovered planets and wild aliens.

But of course, I am taking my friends from Citria wherever I go.

But that's another story.

About the Author

Canadian Illustrator / Author Lizy J. Campbell is a self-taught artist with many interests. She is a mother of two beautiful children and has published over 30 books. She owns a publishing company called The Elite Lizzard Publishing Company in Cornwall, Ontario, Canada. She illustrates children's books and paints pet portraits for people. This is her second sci-fi novel.

SORCERESS'
ABODE
PULP
FOREST
CITY OF THE
CITRUSIANS
TANGARMARINE
TERRITORY
CITRIA
GRAVEYARD